I0684466

GREENBRIER CHRONICLES

A Personal Journey

GREENBRIER CHRONICLES

A Personal Journey

WILLIAM COTTRELL

In memory of my sister, Susie

ACKNOWLEDGEMENTS

My goal in writing this short book was to examine the contentious issues of climate change and environmental well-fare facing Humankind today. Though some key actors are fictional, my account is based in the beautiful setting of the Greenbrier Cove, and intertwined with my personal history. My siblings and other close relatives are an important part of that history. To emphasize that point, I am dedicating *Greenbrier Chronicles* to my late sister, Susan Hill (Susie), who passed in May 2020. She was my closest sibling by age (14 months older) and was a great help in corroborating some key points in our family's history with the Greenbrier area during the past 65 years.

My motivation to accomplish this work was heartily augmented by Vincent Vezza's frequent encouragement. Vincent has been an effective leader of the Cabarrus-Rowan County region of the North Carolina Writers' Network (NCWN) for several years. Without his reinforcement of my efforts, this book would certainly have taken far longer to complete.

My writing was greatly improved by the comments and suggestions of my editor, Alice Osborn. She has the uncanny ability to praise and see room for improvement at the same time. I always listen to her and am better off for it.

Of course, all literary works, however brief, necessitate a diversion from the usual household and family duties. Not merely as time spent in the office writing, but in mental energy deflected from its usual routine. Therefore, I am greatly indebted to my wife, Rebecca, for her appreciation of that need.

Lastly, I can't omit a debt of gratitude to those who sounded the clarion call for action to protect our environment in years past. I feel a special bond with and admiration for Rachel Carson. Her willingness to speak Truth to Power spurred a movement and new way of thinking. The fight continues.

PREFACE

My impending retirement after practicing medicine for more than 39 years in the area of Concord, North Carolina, produced a psychological vacuum that begged for direction. I struggled to create a new identity and develop new goals and passions to fill this void. I fully agreed with Simone de Beauvoir when she averred: "There is only one solution if old age is not to be an absurd parody of our former life, and that is to go on pursing ends that give our existence a meaning." This book is the story of how I developed those new goals and attempted to achieve them.

To tell this story I elected to review my background in chemistry, medicine, and water sports to illustrate how it contributed to my decisions in this personal metamorphosis. You will find I am certainly obsessed with water in its many forms and functions. Though most of the critical activity takes place in the Greenbrier area of the Smokies, I incorporated a whimsical approach involving time travel to reveal events in my formative years and my educational background along with a few historical vignettes.

But how did I come to be concerned with the environment, particularly the controversies surrounding global warming? My chemistry background reinforced my tendency to take an objective analytical approach to physical global problems. Deciphering the causes of global warming and environmental pollution is perhaps the ultimate chemistry and physics dilemma of our age. A more apt question might be, "How could I, given my background, avoid developing a deep concern for these issues?"

The science controversies surrounding pollution and global warming are multivariate nightmares. Although I believe the Intergovernmental Panel on Climate Change (IPCC) scientists offer the best current explanations, the issues are far too complex for the average reader to fully digest. At the same time, reviewing the tactics and political alliances of scientists with connections to conservative think tanks and the fossil fuel industry raises a number of red flags. These loose affiliations bring to mind the wisdom expressed by Upton Sinclair: "It is difficult to get a man to understand something, when his salary depends on his not understanding it." Justifiably, the tale of how some scientists have obfuscated the issues to delay intervention is an important component of my story.

This work is based on real life events of my past. Except for minor variations in timing or names and other details to protect identity, most of the tale might be considered a work of non-fiction, almost an autobiography. But I have stretched that interpretation a bit with the creation of my own think tank in the last few chapters. I have used this tool to reveal the most contentious issues facing our planet today.

Contents

THE GREENBRIER COVE

The unexamined life is not worth living.

—Socrates

Approaching the end of a long career in medicine, I began to ponder what my practice as a physician had meant and how I would be remembered, if I would be remembered at all. I was neither overflowing with egomania and confidence for having successfully met my career goals, nor rueful and melancholy about missed opportunities, although at times, I experienced both emotions. It was a time when I was taking stock of my accomplishments and failures, and contemplating my mortality and all of its ramifications.

I was acutely aware that my best days were behind me by the usual metrics. On most days I still felt mentally and physically on top of my game. But on others I could sense the subtle signs and symptoms that point to the inevitable decline of old age. Why was I flooded with advertisements for male enhancement products on my smart phone? Was it due to some icon I foolishly clicked long ago? Or did the multi-billion dollar advertising industry just have my demographics pin-pointed in their ginormous data bank?

Furthermore, how would they know my ——— was shrinking? By what means did they garner this Information? At any rate, I could not admit I was in need of their products, much less surrender hard-earned money for them.

I think it's important the reader understand the background in which these events unfold, to better interpret their meaning. It would be tempting to label them as nothing but the musings of an affable, but slightly offbeat, aging physician. Indeed, I would be inclined to concur with this interpretation myself were it not for a series of totally unexpected and bizarre encounters I had while staying at my mountain cabin outside of Gatlinburg, Tennessee. What I can say with certainty is that, because of these events, I changed not only the way I viewed my own life and accomplishments, but also how I viewed the human race and the viability of modern civilization itself. But these events would unfold over time. Right now, I needed shelter from the stress of daily life. Only then could I focus on the big questions like, what would I do with myself in retirement? And what would motivate me to get out of bed in the morning? On a grander scale, should I care about the national debt or only my own financial situation? Should I worry about climate change? Or just make sure my heating and cooling system is in good shape? Furthermore, if the sun is going to burn out in five billion years, does it really matter?

To help resolve these issues, I decided to retreat to the mountain cabin my wife and I built in 2006. It is conveniently located a few miles east of Gatlinburg, near the Little Pigeon River, and less than a mile from the Great Smoky Mountains National Park in an area referred to as Greenbrier Cove—so named after a vine called common greenbrier.

Once inside the cabin my stress level drops immediately at least 75 percent. Perhaps this is only because I am physically separated from the usual visual stress triggers. Or perhaps the walls of pine logs or the Douglas firs and rhododendrons outside have some magical soothing effect. No man-made structures, save the road and power lines, are visible. My only concern is the occasional black bear that wanders through the forest looking for something yummy to eat.

Shielded by my armor of solitude and protected by my cabin fortress, I am in my womb of contentment where I can contemplate my most pressing predicaments. Friendship and society—very important, but they can wait. Now is the time I must re-create my identity from within. Should I acquire more hobbies and interests, or just expand and perfect the ones I have? Should I travel more or just become more active in the community? What can I do to maximize preservation of my mind and body? And can you really do anything to prevent shrinkage?

I am very much a man of science. Deductive reasoning, laws of nature and physics, and controlled experimentation are all you need to understand yourself and our evolving Planet Earth. These are the tools we possess to predict the future, plan our lives, and live in harmony with each other and Mother Nature. They never fail to reveal truths that will guide us on our journey. Except when they don't.

I hereby give fair warning to the reader that my perspective may seem a little offbeat and nontraditional. I merely make observations and relate the past as I see it. I am not following any set agenda, political party or academic school of thought. What you see is what you get. On the other hand, I believe I do fit the definition of a concerned humanitarian. I care about Humankind's state of affairs and future well-being. I would even go so far as to say that humans are my favorite mammals. A possible exception might be the river otter. It seems to me they very much enjoy their lives, provided pollution is under control. I confess, however, I haven't had a great deal of up-close personal interactions with otters. So, I'm sticking with humans right now as my favorite.

I could not do justice to this chronicle without relating the haunting and sometimes disturbing history that predates my own familiarity with this region of the country. Archeologists believe various Native American tribes have inhabited this area of the country for at least 12,000 years. That would mean they were here long before the Spaniard Hernando de Soto visited what is now East Tennessee in his vain search for gold and other riches. Evidence indicates that by 1600, the Cherokee had a credible claim over a vast territory that included much of current North and South Carolina, Georgia, Tennessee and Kentucky.

By the late 1600s trading deerskins with white settlers in Virginia and South Carolina was very profitable for the Cherokee people. But, unfortunately, the Cherokee elected to support the French during the French and Indian War (1754 – 1763) and subsequently supported the British during the Revolutionary War (1775 – 1783). This resulted in an adversarial relationship with white settlers. They were "persuaded" to cede most of their ancestral lands to the new settlers and, with the Treaty of New Echota in 1835, were required to surrender all remaining land and relocate to the newly designated Indian Territory in what is now Oklahoma. This mandatory relocation took place in 1838. During the forced removal of the Cherokee by the U.S. Army, it was estimated that 25 percent of the original 16,000 Cherokee died in route. So it goes.

But a number of Cherokee formed a resistance group, who banded together near the current day Cherokee Reservation at Qualla. Between 1875 and 1880, the U.S. government finally recognized the Eastern Band of the Cherokee. However, this was only after the legendary Cherokee Chief, Tsali, and his sons were executed as martyrs. This whole story of the Cherokee's struggle has been depicted in a play, *Unto These Hills* (1950) by Kermit Hunter, which is still being performed as an outdoor drama during the summer months at the Cherokee Mountainside Theatre.

This poignant and evocative history of the Cherokee is well ingrained in my mindset and poses the question: how can a sup-posedly civilized people treat their fellow man so inhumanely? By what legal tenet did the white settlers claim the Cherokee's native territory as their own? The current immigration controversy and coerced removal of the Native American tribes from their homes is irony not lost on me.

Meanwhile, as I contemplate my current situation, I have a need to reconcile my past with the present and future pathways. This might be like predicting the trajectory of a missile by plotting its past locations and speed to extrapolate and predict its future movements. Only by knowing your past can you hope to make credible predictions about tomorrow. This means I need to frequently review important events from years ago and examine their significance for my current situation. This will necessitate some time travel to catch those events.

Today, I am planning on attending Hills Creek Baptist Church, a quaint rural church about a half mile from my cabin on the Little Pigeon River. It was this very church I attended in 1959 while vacationing with my family in the Greenbrier area as a ten-year-old. At that time, I was working on a perfect attendance record for my home church of First United Methodist Church of Concord, a 90-minute drive away. To avoid an attendance breach, my father dropped me off at the Baptist church on Sunday morning. As a result, I was awarded a perfect attendance prize: a handy pocket-sized bird manual with pictures and descriptions of more than 200 birds east of the Rockies. On the inside flap the inscription read: "To Billy Cottrell, an outstanding Junior boy. From Mrs. B.D. Dunlap, October 4, 1959." After sixty years I still treasure this relic.

I enter the little church surreptitiously hoping not to attract attention—hard to do when the total congregation numbers only 30 people. Soon the minister walks over to my pew to shake my hand. I explain I am celebrating a 60th anniversary for attending his church as a child. He seems pleased.

The first 30 minutes of the service consists of country-gospel songs played by a trio of guitarists including the minister. I am impressed by the quality and spiritual energy of the performers.

This is followed by the usual church announcements and a vigorously delivered sermon. I feel strangely out of place but garner a deep appreciation for the minister and his church. Small-time Baptist churches and old-time religion are alive and well in rural America.

So, what is my overarching goal with this attendance six decades after my only other visit? I'm not sure, but I locate my 60-year-old bird manual and write: "Attended Hills Creek Baptist Church, July 12, 2019," below the date, October 4, 1959. It just seemed the right thing to do.

I must admit I don't attend church as regularly as I did in my younger days. Sadly, I lost some of the motivation I had as a younger man. Curiously, this experience awakened a renewed interest in this nostalgic time of my life. We were different then. Families were more traditional. And our country's global image and challenges were different. I am currently attempting to view the world through a multi-cultural prism. Does this make me a better person? Or does it lessen my ability to focus? Furthermore, what will the role of these modest rural churches be in helping to solve global problems? I really don't know, but I feel certain that they will survive and continue to have an influence.

It's clear from these vignettes that this mountain area has been intimately involved, not only in my personal growth, but also in the early development of the country. This may also help explain why such curious and foreboding events took place in the Greenbrier Cove area of the Smokies and how they would transform the way I viewed our collective futures.

THE BEGINNING

The most insidious influence on the young is not violence,
drugs, tobacco, drink, or sexual perversion, but our pursuit of
the trivial and our tolerance of the third rate.

— Eric Anderson

There is nothing in my personal history to suggest I was transported to earth by aliens or created by a mad scientist in their laboratory. According to my parents' autobiography, I was born in Oak Ridge, Tennessee, (also known as the Atomic City or Secret City) on February 20, 1949, the third of five children. This theory is corroborated by photographic evidence that appears to be authentic. It is also compatible with hearsay of friends and relatives, and quasi-legal documents such as baby books. Anyone with a "birther" theory of my origins would have an uphill battle. However, given that some people deny the Holocaust ever happened, I guess there's no guarantee that someone couldn't attempt to make that claim about me.

Neuroscientists tell us that memories are not created by new nerve cells (neurons) or by new connections (synapses) between nerve cells but, rather, by the facilitation of pre-existing connections and pathways between cells. I can vaguely recall an undersized, white, government-issued home on Quincey Avenue in Oak Ridge. I can visualize an ironing board in the living room and a tiny bedroom with a paper plate that held all my known financial assets. A toy pistol that used real caps was my favorite possession. A mother and two sisters are there; a father and brothers don't make the memory threshold until later. Clearly these neural pathways are fading. And how can anyone really tell the difference between a true memory and imaginings and recreations of previous impressions?

In 1953, our family moved from Oak Ridge to the community of Farragut, where my father purchased a 3,500-square-foot brick house with 13 acres of farmland. My memories of this house are decidedly stronger than the first, as we lived here until 1966, when I became a high school senior. This house was on the previous homesite of Archibald Roane, the second governor of Tennessee (1801 – 1804), though there were no remains of Roane's home. A circular driveway, more than two acres of yards, majestic silver maples, pecan trees, and a small orchard distinguished our home from others. It was bordered on the south by Turkey Creek and surrounded by farmland. Across Admiral Drive sat an old, dilapidated barn slated for demolition, and a modest, one-level home without an indoor bathroom. As young kids, my siblings and I marveled at the beauty and simplicity of the outdoor john. Our neighbors even allowed us to try it out. However, this house with its outbuilding mysteriously disappeared a year or so after our arrival.

Our new home was much bigger than the Oak Ridge house and had many interesting features. The second story had four nice-sized bedrooms and two full bathrooms. The main floor had a spacious living room, a kitchen, dining room, den, foyer, and bonus room. There was a full, unfinished basement that included a huge play area, my father's workshop, and a coal bin with a stoker and furnace to heat water for the radiators throughout the house. Connecting the top floor to the basement was a narrow laundry chute for delivering dirty laundry to the washing machine. It was just the right size to allow a young child to descend without harm when parents were not watching.

When I think of my childhood, images from this house still haunt my memory. There are many stories to be told that may help explain my idiosyncrasies and obsessions. But first, I must return to the mountains at Greenbrier to explain my early acquaintance with this area.

My sister, Susie, and I agree that our family's first visit to the Greenbrier area was in the summer of 1954. My father learned through a work acquaintance that the Barbers owned a cabin on the Little Pigeon River just outside the park that they were willing to rent to us for a week. I can vividly recall the tiny brown cabin with cedar shake siding near the river's edge. A lush carpet of pine needles among the white pines, eastern hemlocks, and Douglas firs greatly softened any loud noises and gave the area an aura of enchantment. At the same time, the river water negotiating its way over and around the protruding rocks made its own visual and acoustic contribution to the beguiling sensation of other-worldliness. How could I have known this area of the mountains would loom so prominently in my future? It soon became a fixture of our family vacations.

At five years old, I knew very little about the park or the story of its creation. I assumed it was there forever. The park was in fact created on June 15, 1934, when the U.S. government allotted the needed funds to purchase the land. The infrastructure, built by the Civilian Conservation Corps (CCC) in the late 1930s was, therefore, still quite new on my initial visit.

The Greenbrier area of the Great Smoky Mountains National Park is near the park's northern border, almost due north of the town of Cherokee on its southern border. Its borders are the Greenbrier Pinnacle on the east, and the lower slopes of Mt. Le Conte on the west. The Middle Prong of the Little Pigeon River runs through the center of the cove. As the river runs north and crosses U.S. 321, the land becomes much flatter. At this point, the river valley is known as Emerts Cove, named after the family of Frederick Emert who settled there around 1784. Emerts Cove is actually an extension of Greenbrier Cove and considered part of the Greenbrier area. The cabin we rented was just off Emerts Cove Road, within easy walking distance of the park.

William Whaley was the first settler of Greenbrier Cove in 1810. His brother, Middleton, settled in the nearby Glades community. Between them, they had 16 children, of whom 10 were boys. Middleton's son Aaron had 11 children, seven of whom were sons. Needless to say, the Whaley name was prevalent in those early days. It still is today, along with Ogle, McCarter, and Huskey. These were highly resourceful, rugged individuals who survived not only through their primitive hunting and farming skills, but also thanks to a culture of mutual assistance in times of special need. Maximum use was made of plants and animals. After using almost all of a hog's body parts for food, the bladder was blown up and used as a toy ball. Eggshells were crushed and recycled as chicken food. And corn stalks were used for silage, fodder, and corn meal. The shucks, once woven, were valuable for seating chairs. Recycling was a way of life.

Far and away the biggest event in the history of Greenbrier Cove was the federal government's taking of residents' homes in the 1930s to create the park. Old-timers grieved this event for more than 70 years. Unlike the slightly better known Cades Cove, about an hour's drive away, no families were allowed to remain in Greenbrier Cove. This resulted in the relocation of about 1,000 people from 150 families.

Only vaguely aware of these events during our initial visits to Emerts Cove, my family was fixated on enjoying the natural beauty of the park's rivers, trails, and bucolic vistas. Eventually, we would learn more about the colorful history as we met more locals and much later built our own log cabin.

The summer of 1955 was also memorable for several reasons. We continued to rent the same cabin. The best swimming hole, however, was a rocky 200-yard walk upstream, where a natural bend in the river, along with strategically placed boulders, created a reasonably deep and tranquil swimming hole—it was bordered by a smooth beach on one side, and a huge rock for sunbathing or diving on the other. Above and below were Class II rapids—good for tubing, but not so great for swimming. It was at this spot, more than 65 years ago, where I swam my first strokes. I can show you the exact location this happened. Just below this site, Susie had a more harrowing experience among the rapids.

I can still visualize it clearly. Destabilized by slippery river rocks and a strong current, Susie clung desperately to a huge river rock as the rushing water pulled her legs and torso downstream. A nearby man saved her from a possible rough tumble down the rapids. Although I don't believe her life was ever in serious danger, we both remember this childhood accident as a momentous occasion to be retold with a little more drama each time.

Back at our new home in Farragut, we soon faced a much more serious situation. I was playing on the bridge over Turkey Creek, about 200 yards from our house, with my younger brother, four-year-old Scotty, and an older neighborhood friend, seven-year-old Rogers, when Scotty suddenly fell off the eight-foot wooden bridge and landed on the rocks below. Amazingly, he walked up the muddy slope to the road unassisted while softly crying. Right away I could see this was serious. One side of his face was covered with mud streaked with blood. What type of first aid maneuver was most appropriate? I was only six, so I elected to run back to the house to get my mother, who was caring for my youngest brother, Steve, who was one years old.

The next day, Scotty underwent an emergent neurosurgical procedure to implant a plastic plate inside the defect in his skull. He made a full physical recovery, but had to wear a protective football helmet for several months. There was no indication his mental abilities were impaired by this accident. Years later, he graduated from West Point, ranking 14th out of 930 cadets. At the time, we were just glad he had no complications from the accident.

After this episode, the 1950s proved to be a crisis-free and family-oriented affair. *The Adventures of Ozzie and Harriet* had nothing over us. I entered first grade at Farragut Elementary in September 1955 without any kindergarten or other preparation. Far from precocious, it took me several years to define myself as a good student. My family looked forward to our annual week in the mountains but, of course, most of our time was spent around our relatively new home in Farragut.

These were peaceful times on a worldwide level as well. Joseph Stalin died in 1953, and the Korean conflict came to a close that same year. As a matter of fact, scientist William Tunstal-Pedoe declared April 11, 1954 the most boring day in history based on the results of his search engine, True Knowledge. Apparently, no one of great importance was born or died that day, and no major newsworthy events occurred—a useful fact to remember if you like to impress friends with trivia.

On the other hand, it wasn't long after this uneventful time that school children were rehearsing how to deal with a possible nuclear attack. Having your own bomb shelter became avant-garde. Around the same time, the French defeat in Vietnam on May 7, 1954 led directly to increased involvement of U.S. forces against the revolutionaries led by Ho Chi Minh. We all know what happened over the next 20 years. Undoubtedly, the seeds of conflict and turmoil are frequently planted during years that appear calm but, in reality, have a lot happening beneath the surface.

I believe this same phenomenon evident in world politics is also relevant on a personal level. During tranquil periods of life, wheels are churning internally. A child or young adult is forming behavior patterns, neural pathways are being created and facilitated in the brain based on personal experiences, and the seeds of future conflicts and challenges are being planted. In other words, character develops for better or worse. The initial trajectory of life's journey is being formed but with very little outward evidence. To understand events in later life it is helpful to examine the early life. Perhaps this will help me interpret the mysterious encounters I had in Greenbrier Cove in old age.

After my brother's close call with the bridge accident, my younger years were devoid of any major physical or emotional trauma. At times I even worried I had it too easy, that at some point a major catastrophe or shock might befall my family or me. I also worried I could be perceived by my peers as too innocent or prudish to be credible. This identity angst was not too serious as a 10-year-old, but became a bit more inured as I entered my teens. I was acutely aware of my status and occasionally might adopt some anti-authoritarian philosophy or engage in some token rebellious antic to embellish my hipster image. At age 15, I assisted two friends in rolling a neighbor's yard with toilet paper on Halloween's Eve. When apprehended, however, I apologized and even assisted with the cleanup. My role as the neighborhood Fonzie was far from assured.

When I turned 16 in 1965, my mother planned a surprise birthday party for me at our house in Farragut. A good friend was assigned as a decoy to delay my arrival home from school so guests could arrive at the house without my knowing. I was completely and somewhat pleasantly surprised by the whole affair. Good work, Mom! No harm in a little party, even if it was a little traditional. Then I opened a gift she carefully wrapped, a vinyl LP disc from 1957, "At the Hop," by Danny and the Juniors. Keep in mind this was 1965—The Beatles, The Doors, The Rolling Stones, and Bob Dylan were creating a new sound, with which I had a strong identity. "At the Hop" was from another universe. I was so embarrassed that I immediately hid the record under my chair so no one would see it. But thanks anyway, Mom, I know you tried.

Despite the bland environment of my upbringing, I am convinced there were some important struggles and developments on an inconspicuous and subliminal level. What were those critical episodes in my early life that made me what I am? Furthermore, if I compare myself to Santiago, the Andalusian shepherd boy in *The Alchemist* by Paul Coelho, what treasure was I pursuing, and how would I go about creating my Personal Legend? To answer these and related questions, I must go back to 1959 when I was a naïve 10-year-old, decidedly clueless about the vicissitudes of life. I was propelled down the road by a mysterious force, believing that my pot of gold was in easy reach.

The hula hoop craze, which began in 1958, was in full force in my hometown by 1959. I began to witness the antics of other kids as they experimented with this delightful toy. A few made bodacious claims of completing an unprecedented number of revolutions. Not to be outdone, I came home from my fourth-grade class one afternoon in early 1959 and began my hula hoop marathon in the living room around 3:30. I was still going at 5:30 when my father got home from work. Finally, around 7:30, I gave it up after I far surpassed any record that I knew of by anybody from my school. My mother called the *Knoxville News Sentinel* to report this miraculous feat. A short article appeared the next day announcing my accomplishment. A day or two later, reporters from the paper arrived at my school to see me in action. For a short while I was walking on air. I seemed to have achieved a sort of semi-celebrity status. With a hula- hoop title under my belt, could fame and fortune be far behind? Unfortunately, it all came crashing down a few weeks later.

The *Knoxville News Sentinel* decided to sponsor an all-comers hula hoop endurance contest at the University of Tennessee sports arena. It began on a Friday evening around 6:00. If your hula hoop hit the ground, you were out. Last man standing was the winner. By around 10:00, I was one of about 20 finalists. The judges, however, made the decision to halt the contest and reconvene the next evening for the finale. It must have been past their bedtime. So, Saturday evening we began again, but with only the finalist competing. After about an hour or so, my mother, believing I must be hungry, handed me a pack of crackers. As I reached out to grab them, my elbow caught the hoop and caused it to spiral down to my knees. I desperately attempted to shimmy it back up to my waist with some frantic body gyrations. But I had not really practiced that maneuver. It didn't work. Along with the hoop went my dream of fame and fortune. Looking back, I can now see how these events made an impression on me. First of all, they gave me an inkling of what success and notoriety might feel like. But, more importantly, they taught me about the thin margins between success and failure and the importance of humility. These lessons would make me sadder but wiser, and more prepared to compete in future struggles in an objective manner. But really, what good is a lousy pack of crackers anyway?

In addition to my hula hoop escapade and my perfect attendance record garnered by visiting Hills Creek Baptist Church in Emerts Cove in 1959, another important event made it quite a noteworthy year. In August of that summer, my father drove our family north to Maine where we stayed for a week at the rustic resort Mingo Springs on Rangeley Lake. My parents were co-owners of Mingo Springs and its sister resort, the Cobossee. Normally humble and well-behaved, my siblings and I couldn't resist the temptation of stealing a snack or two from behind the lunch counter, due to our regrettable sense of entitlement.

The big event for me that year was learning to waterski. This was accomplished by sitting on the edge of the dock while holding on to a ski rope attached to an accelerating motorboat. I remember the water as shockingly cold. (Years later, I googled water temperature for Maine lakes in this area—the warmest they get is about 62 – 63 degrees Fahrenheit. That would explain it.)

On the way back home, we stopped in Cambridge, Massachusetts, to visit my mother's uncle, Doctor Avery Ashdown, fondly known as Uncle Avery to my siblings and me. He was a professor at Massachusetts Institute of Technology

(MIT) and also a bachelor who lived on campus, so of course he arranged for us to stay in a student dormitory. Not an earth-shattering event, but the novelty of staying in a college dorm as a 10-year-old left an impression. MIT later named a dormitory in his honor, The Ashdown House.

At age 10, I was only vaguely aware that, in 1959, Fidel Castro and his communist rebels ousted Fulgencio Batista in Cuba just 90 miles south of our country's southern border, or that the Dalai Lama was forced to flee Tibet and take up residency in India. I do well recall that Alaska and Hawaii became our 49th and 50th states. But none of these political events had much effect on me personally.

More relevant was the peaceful feeling of the late '50s captured by some of the top Billboard songs. "The Three Bells" by the Browns, "Lonely Boy" by Paul Anka, and "Dream Lover" by Bobby Darin, suggested an age of innocence and harmony. Or perhaps that's merely how we prefer to interpret it. The '60s would change all of that.

One last memory from that quaint mid-century era was almost too good to be true for a fifth grader. We had a record number of school days missed because of heavy snow. The weather log for nearby Knoxville recorded a total of 56 inches of snow in the winter of 1959 – 1960. Our community, however, had a total of 54 inches. This meant not only a lot of time out of school, but also hockey games on frozen ponds using a piece of frozen cow dung for a puck and a tree branch for a hockey stick. Impromptu sledding parties with a bonfire and roasted marshmallows at the top of Admiral Drive created idyllic memories of childhood that were meant to be savored. That year's collective experiences could only foster good karma. So far as a 10-year-old, I had no idea what my Personal Legend might be. But the signs were optimistic. As a historical footnote, no winter to date has ever surpassed 1959 – 1960 for total snowfall in East Tennessee, and none has even come close.

THE SIXTIES

People today are still living off the table scraps of the sixties.
They are still being passed around—the music and the ideas.

—Bob Dylan

The decade of the 1960s is frequently singled out as a time of change and controversy. Was it a time of disrespect for traditional religious values, or of a sincere search to rediscover Humankind's true relationship with God? A time to demonstrate that science and engineering could solve all our planet's problems? Or a time we realized the need to respect the forces of nature? A time our country demonstrated its ability to save the world by spreading its form of government across the globe? Or was it a time we realized that, by its inherent nature, a true democracy is more likely to arise from within than imposed from outside? A time to turn on, tune out, and drop out? Or a time of creativity in the arts and a sincere search for meaning? As we who experienced the decade all know, it was all of the above. But I prefer to value the decade for its positive attributes.

On a personal level I transitioned from a naïve prepubescent 11-year-old to a full grown, and somewhat less naïve 21-year-old, still trying to discover what his Personal Legend might be. A number of adolescent experiences were giving me helpful clues. Were these excursions predetermined by some cosmic force? Or were they expressions of my free will? It amuses me to recount some of these events and attempt to answer that question.

Annual visits to the Greenbrier area of the Smokies were well established by 1960, but the lodging arrangements varied at times. We began renting a more spacious and upscale cabin several hundred yards upstream from the Barbers, owned by the Bearskin Motel with the descriptive name of Non-Monotonous. This mountain hideaway had an outdoor kitchen and an expansive patio overlooking the river, which made for easy access to the swimming hole only a few rocky steps away. The nearby Class II river rapids were a popular recreational feature, and the right size for shooting with an old inner tube. Depending on the size of the tube and the joy seeker's body, your butt could take a beating. But that never slowed us down. As we grew more adventurous, we would ask someone to drive us upstream to the park to ensure a longer and more exciting ride.

The other activity of note was hiking on one of the many park trails. Our favorite was the Alum Bluff Cave Trail leading to the peak of Mt. Le Conte. About an 11-mile round trip, it required at least five or six hours due to the steep grade in many sections of the trail. The sycamore and hardwood forest at the trailhead merges into the birch and lacy hemlocks forest of the middle section and ultimately leads to the spruce-fir forest near the top. This would be similar to the changes seen when traveling from Georgia to Maine. I will never forget the first time I viewed the plush mountain side through the bluish haze from the rocky ledge at the peak. It would soften the heart of even a hard-core urbanite.

While these mountain excursions were usually the highlight of my year in the early '60s, I simultaneously enjoyed some success in unrelated areas. After playing midget football in the falls of '61 and '62, I realized it was unlikely I would garner great fame or notoriety in that arena. It did, however, pique my interest in physical fitness. Concepts of speed and physical strength suddenly became important. As my coach noted, I was usually in front of the pack when the team ran laps around the football field for conditioning. Thus, at age 13, I adopted a home fitness routine that included push-ups, pull-ups, burpees, and running. As a result, exercise became engrained in my mindset at an early age. Working out became a habit—burdensome at times, but usually just a part of my daily schedule.

I also experienced moderate success with music, especially the piano. Though never as prodigious on the instrument as my older sister, Karen, I did master a few of the classics. Chopin and Rachmaninoff were within my reach. Later in my teens, the acoustic guitar replaced the piano as my preferred instrument. Sadly, my piano skills have diminished over time. But I do still enjoy listening to the piano classics.

What did my fascination with physical fitness and music have to do with each other? I'm really not sure. Perhaps it was pure coincidence. On the other hand, I believe that success in both arenas depends on a routine of practice and repetition, and, importantly, mental discipline. Possibly because of this realization, I developed the philosophy that tedious repetition could help me achieve all my goals, and therefore I could find my treasure. Who needs talent? What is talent? Thus, my mindset was heavily influenced by these early endeavors. But did I choose them? Or was I predestined to behave as I did?

To enhance my exercise routine at home, I acquired a set of barbells, 110 pounds total, for the Christmas of '63. Two 25-pound plates were added the next year to make 160 pounds in all. These weights remained in the basement where I did a routine of six or seven exercises several times a week. Later in high school, my routine included doing 20 to 25 full squats with 155 pounds on my back. Possibly my best exercise, it did present some logistical problems. This weight was slightly more than I could clean and jerk at the time. Without a squat rack or other equipment, and with no one else to assist me, I had to devise a unique system to raise the weights on my shoulders. I would put the barbell on the basement steps, at about the four-foot level, and then pull one end off the side of the step so at least one foot of the bar was precariously hanging off the edge. Then I would duck my head under the bar and slowly slide it onto my shoulders. After completing the exercise, I would reverse the process and slowly slide the bar onto the same stair step. Fortunately, I never had an accident with this technique. The wooden stairs, however, did develop some serious grooves from wear and tear. Luckily for me, no one seemed too upset about that.

It's true that tedious repetition with both physical exercise and music practice took up a big chunk of my time and energy in my teenage years. But there were also some key exploits that left deep impressions on me, helping to shape my outlook. Self-analysis can only shed a dim light on how these ventures affected my life in later years. By reviewing a few of them, perhaps I can see some noteworthy patterns taking shape.

I continued to visit the Greenbrier for at least a week each summer, but other trips were also quite memorable. For example, in 1963, our whole family, minus my eldest sister who was working at Mingo Springs in Maine, took a three-week road trip out west in our '62 Chevrolet Bel Air station wagon. My father built a plywood food cabinet to fit in the back of the wagon. This came in handy when we camped at state parks, which included Tenkiller (Oklahoma), Palo Duro Canyon (Texas), and Bluewater (New Mexico). I well remember visiting aunts and uncles, Knots Berry Farm, and Salt Lake City, where my father had a nuclear safety meeting. To this day, I remember a major concern was finding a good spot to do pull-ups, my favorite exercise. A stairwell, maybe, convenient ledge, or monkey bars were okay. Shower curtain rods were not okay. Usually I could find a spot, but not all campsites and motels were pull-up friendly.

It seemed that each year garnered increased drama for me as the decade progressed. For example, in the spring of '64, my father had to undergo a major operation for a tumor. He chose to inform us that he merely had a tiny "polyp" removed.

That same summer, we faced an issue with our usual mountain excursion. Neither the Barbers' cabin nor Non-Monotonous were available, so we elected to rent an old farmhouse about a quarter-mile downstream. This was fine with us, but it made the walk to the swimming hole a bit longer.

During this week in Greenbrier, my father decided to run with me to assist his recuperation from surgery. This was an ambitious plan, as I was a distance runner on the high school track team. After about a quarter-mile, he had to stop. I felt badly for him and maybe even a little guilty. At the same time, I wondered what I could do to avoid the same misfortune. My siblings and I were pretty sure that it was more than just a little polyp.

Serious health issues in a family tend to raise questions about cause, in particular, the role of environment versus genes. As I've learned, this is not always an easy distinction—this is because the environment heavily influences genetic expression. It seems genetic/environment interaction is everywhere. So, the answer is not simple.

The next drama that summer took place at Camp Pellissippi, our Boy Scout camp at Lake Norris, part of the Clinch River system. A water carnival was held on Saturday, the last full day of camp. Canoeing and rowing events were conducted on the open waters of Lake Norris. But the individual and relay swim races, along with the greased watermelon contest, took place in a protected area referred as to as the "crib." A square roughly 50 feet per side, the crib was bordered on each side by wooden docks, and had wooden plank flooring.

It seemed we won the medley relay race, but were disqualified because the counselors claimed I left the dock before touching the incoming swimmer. No instant replay available. Bummer! My next event was the underwater swim. Most competitors did two to three lengths of the crib underwater. I managed to do four lengths and win the top spot in the event. This was a great boost to our troop and helped us win top honors overall. It was also sweet revenge for a possible unfair call on the relay. Once again, I thought I might possess a unique talent of some note that would merit a degree of fame and respect. Unfortunately, other than a brief feeling of elation, this didn't prove to be the case. Underwater swimming is not a standard event in high school swim meets. Plus, our school didn't even have a swim team.

Years later, while a medical resident in Gainesville, Florida, I swam a total of three and a half laps (seven lengths) underwater at my apartment community's pool. This is about 100 yards. In case this seems unbelievable, I googled "World Record for Underwater Swimming" and found the record is held by Dave Mullins, who swam 244 meters (268 yards). So, at 100 yards, Mullins was just getting warmed up. I am glad to have the ability to swim pretty far underwater but, so far, I haven't found any special use for this talent.

I have already discussed the surprise birthday party my mother planned for me in February 1965. That party gave the year an auspicious beginning but not much insight into further developments. In July of that year, our family again rented Non-Monotonous, my favorite cabin, for a week. The patio's outdoor kitchen sometimes doubled as an extra bedroom. One evening, I was invited to play cards with the teenagers from a nearby cabin. I developed a crush on one of the girls staying there. The next day, we walked along the river, holding hands while developing a romantic bond. Unfortunately, my family's weeklong stay was ending in a few days, so that was that. At 16, I was inexperienced in romance, but enthralled to have had a brief but meaningful fling. For several weeks, I brooded and hoped against all reason that I might by chance run into her again. Eventually, I had to admit what happened. My normal logical thought process was vulnerable. It seems that strong desires and wishes can be a catalyst for irrational thinking. But then, where would we be without strong desires and wishes? The summer was far from over.

That August, I went to a Boy Scouts-sponsored aquatic school at Camp Buck Toms on the Tennessee River system for a week. This included training in all types of water sports, i.e., swimming, rowing, canoeing, life-saving, mile swim, and so on. After passing all tests, I became a certified Scout lifeguard. This was a nice perk, but the best was yet to come.

During our free time at aquatic school, four of us concocted plans for another water adventure. Why not complete a 50-plus-mile canoe trip after finishing our training at Camp Buck Toms, and earn that Scouting distinction? We started at the Chilhowee Dam on the Little Tennessee River, and ended at Concord Boat Dock on Fort Loudon Lake, part of the Tennessee River system, after a five-day journey. This included one night of camping at Fort Loudon, and the necessity of paddling through the lock system of Fort Loudon Dam. This feat did not require any supreme strength or specialized training but, rather, basic navigation and canoeing skills for a five-day stretch. The benefit of this excursion was not merely earning the 50-mile canoeing award, but gaining a broader perspective of our abilities. If we could canoe 50 miles, why not try 150 or 500 miles? It was the perfect way to end the summer before my junior year of high school.

The following summer of 1966, my parents decided to sell our house near the high school and move to a smaller house in a middle-class neighborhood. I was not happy with this decision at the time, as I equated this house and surrounding acreage with everything good about my childhood. But now I understand. The bigger house and yards required a lot of care. As my sisters left for college and my brothers and I approached that same age, it made sense for my parents to downsize.

If I ever have a chance to enter this house again, I would like to inspect the doorway between the kitchen and den. About 60 years ago, I tossed a 50-cent piece up in the air when it became lodged in a crack between the doorframe and the wall. There was no way to retrieve it without tearing off the frame. Unless the doorframe has been totally replaced, the half-dollar should still be there. So, in addition to having a nostalgic visit, perhaps I could impress the current owners with this trivia. Maybe I could even retrieve the coin.

Around the same time our family moved, I began a 12-week adventure as an exchange student to Norway with the American Field Service (AFS) program. In early June, I flew to New York and was joined by several hundred other high school students as we set sail on the *Seven Seas*, a refurbished World War II cargo ship, for Rotterdam. Some students had signed up for a whole year. Many, however, like me, were going just for the summer. We were all assigned to a family in a European country. Those students staying for a year were sent to a language camp for two weeks before reaching their ultimate destination.

As a summer student, I had no overwhelming need to become fluent in Norwegian. But I accepted the challenge to give it a good try. I crammed during the ten-day boat trip to learn as much as I could. When my Norwegian father picked me up at the train station in Oslo, I regurgitated a few rehearsed lines in "Norsk." Unfortunately, my soft voice was drowned out by background noise, and he had no idea what I said. I never did become fluent in Norwegian, but by the end of the summer, I picked up a number of phrases. Nearly everyone I met in Norway spoke English anyway. I do believe they warmly acknowledged my efforts to embrace Norsk.

I consider my summer in Norway as perhaps the best experience of my adolescent years. It was mind-expanding and humbling at the same time. I can condense the essence of that experience into two short vignettes.

I attended the Norwegian Boy Scout camp at Seljord with my two Norwegian brothers, Lorentz-Peter and Stein, in July. I received a warm reception and respect from the other Scouts.

However, eventually I was asked the inevitable question: how did I feel about my country's involvement in Vietnam? Remember, this was 1966. I gave the most sincere and middle-of-the-road answer I could conjure up at the moment. The U.S. was there merely to assist the Vietnamese people in determining their own form of government. That was not an unusual position to take at the time. Some might argue so even today. But immediately after speaking in front of my peace-loving Norwegian friends, the weakness of that argument hit me like a blow to the chin. If we want the Vietnamese to determine their own form of government, do they really need our help? Obviously, one's thought process can be greatly influenced by the intellectual and political milieu of their environment.

The second story concerns my Norwegian family's visit to Drobak, a resort town on the Oslo Fjord, toward the end of summer. My Norwegian brother and I spent an entire hour in the fjord before getting out. The water temperature was seventeen degrees Celsius (roughly sixty three degrees Fahrenheit) similar to the lakes in Maine. I felt like an icicle. I'm pretty sure the only reason I survived was that I was seventeen. But such experiences affect your frame of reference. If anybody ever asks me today if the lake or pool water in North Carolina is cold, I can only truthfully respond, *no, not really.* Compared to the Oslo Fjord, it's quite pleasant. I returned to the States just in time to begin my senior year at Farragut. It was a wonderful summer, but it was time to get back to work. This was the only time in 65 years that I failed to make it to Greenbrier area. But it was well worth it.

My senior year of high school was somewhat anti-climactic. I ran on the two-mile relay team that broke the school record in this event, but that record was soon blasted to smithereens. I also was asked to be a commencement speaker at graduation because the valedictorian declined the opportunity. That was bittersweet. The biggest event was preparing for the next level of education by taking the ACT test and filling out applications. Actually, unlike students today, who apply to several schools, I applied to only one, the University of Tennessee. My logic was very simple: I could only go to one school. UT would do just fine.

The University of Tennessee was a big state school with something for everyone. UT had many excellent professors and academically strong departments. There was also a significant fraternity and sorority presence and a distinct social hierarchy. Fundamentalists, right-wingers, liberals, and hippies were also well represented. Students had ample opportunities to pursue their desired path. The goal was to find a comfortable niche. Mine was to become the chemistry and math nerd. This wasn't as terrible as it sounds. As a result, I acquired the job of tutoring several attractive female students from my calculus class. I dated one student for a few months. It was a close call but I wasn't ready for a long-term relationship. I elected not to join a fraternity. It didn't seem an essential ingredient of my Personal Legend. Even so, I was generally accepted by most, but not all, of the social hierarchy. I suppose I was a social chameleon. Although that generally worked out fine, there were at least a few occasions on which I was a little embarrassed by my affiliation with some of the student population.

"John" was a quiet and shy student who lived in my dorm. He had a slight build, was pale, un-athletic, and not a stylish dresser—clearly low on the social pecking order. But he did have one area of expertise: trains. John was a railroad enthusiast, highly knowledgeable about all aspects of train travel including history, engine types, cars, and quite a few actual schedules. Several students found John's eccentricity amusing. They would enter his room and ask him a variety of questions about trains just to push his buttons. John would always answer seriously and accurately. I'm not sure he realized he was being used. Although I didn't initiate these unkind displays of condescension, I am ashamed I did nothing to prevent them.

The end of the decade found me halfway through my junior year of college. The exact nature of my Personal Legend was still elusive, although several themes seemed to be relevant. The use of math as well as quantitative and qualitative analysis to solve chemistry problems created a mindset that was widely applicable to other areas. My fascination with water, based on my recreational encounters, was only reinforced by my study of chemistry. Was any compound more important to life and organic reactions than H_2O? Further, was any substance more important in the history and to the future of Humankind than the universal solvent? In addition, my love affairs with the acoustic guitar and personal fitness were helpful in achieving a degree of psychological balance and stability. It seemed wise to view your ego like eggs. It is preferable not to put all your eggs or ego in one basket. Eggos, however, are best kept in one place.

The country was strongly divided in the late '60s, mostly over the Vietnam War, but also over racial and economic issues. Most people were either right or left, for the war or against. I sometimes got pegged as a freewheeling hippie. My hair was moderately long, and I sported wire-rimmed glasses and occasional bell-bottomed jeans. But I was drug-free and about as socially innocent as one could be. So, this designation by the Right amused more than angered me. Political controversy can bring out the best and the worst in people. I guess that sums up the 1960s.

THE AGE OF AQUARIUS

Anything else you are interested in is not going to happen if you can't breathe the air and drink the water. Don't sit this one out. Do something. You are by accident of fate, alive at an absolutely critical moment in the history of our planet.

—Carl Sagan

The Age of Aquarius is an astrological term denoting the roughly 2,150-year time period during which the vernal equinox moves out of the constellation Pisces into the constellation Aquarius. Or something like that. There's disagreement among experts about when that actually happens. Many believe it occurred in the 20th century. On a personal level, I think it began when the 5th Dimension released the album, *The Age of Aquarius*, in 1969. The eponymous song was actually a medley of two songs from the musical, *Hair*, which opened on Broadway in 1968 and became sort of a theme song for the baby boomer generation. Along with songs like "Peace Train" by Yusuf/Cat Stevens, it encouraged people to think love was on the rise and a better day was just around the corner. Sure, I know many people don't fall for that romantic and overly optimistic pitch. But if you can't put a positive spin on life, why bother? Occasionally, avant-garde artistic trends can pave the way for realpolitik diplomacy and policies.

The Age of Aquarius also ushered in a greater awareness of pollution and spurned a new interest in environmentalism. The 1969 fire in the Cuyahoga River in Cleveland and other eco-disasters paved the way for creating Earth Day on April 22, 1970, now a global holiday.

Earth Day successfully channeled some of the energy of the anti-war movement to help put environmental concerns on the front page. It seems to have been successful.

Much of the popular music of the early '70s reflects the growing focus on environmental issues. My favorite is "Big Yellow Taxi" by Joni Mitchell (1970); there's also "Don't Go Near the Water" by the Beach Boys (1971), "Mercy Me" by Marvin Gaye (1971), and "Out in the Country" by Three Dog Night (1973)—all of these songs focus on great concern for the health of our environment, the Planet Earth.

The 1970s saw 23 federal environmental acts become law. These included the Clean Air Act (1970), the Clean Water Act (1972), the Endangered Species Act (1973), and the Safe Drinking Water Act (1974). Some call the '70s the golden age of environmental law. This legislative activism was complimented by the creation of activist organizations like Friends of the Earth (1969) and Greenpeace (1971). All this made us feel like a new age was dawning.

Concern for the environment and chemical pollution had actually been gaining steam since the early '60s. In 1962, US biologist and environmentalist Rachael Carson released *Silent Spring*, the classic work that started the environmental movement. Carson's most significant contribution was pointing out how man-made chemicals, such as the insecticide DDT, when applied widely, resulted in a host of undesirable side effects. Not only do insects frequently develop a resistance to the chemical and become even more difficult to control, but the chemicals themselves become incorporated into the food chain, which includes humans.

As Carson's biographer, Linda Lear, stated, "In the 1960s, however, the multi-million- dollar industrial chemical industry was not about to allow a former government editor without a PhD or institutional affiliation known for her lyrical books on the sea, undermine public confidence in its products or to question its integrity." Many tried to portray her as a "bird and bunny lover" and a romantic who had overstepped the bounds of her gender and her science.

Ms. Carson died 18 months after publication of *Silent Spring*, but she lived long enough to see how her book was beginning to change how people viewed their interaction with the natural world. It spurred a grassroots movement that demanded environmental protection at the federal and state levels. In other words, it played a vital role in setting the stage for the environmental activism of the '70s.

How did the Age of Aquarius and the environmental movement affect me personally? I understood the concept of achieving global harmony and the need for a cleaner environment, but I can't claim this caused any major change in my lifestyle at the time. I was still an impoverished student scraping by. But I did appreciate the aesthetics of a changing world. It now seemed obvious that technology and industry couldn't solve all Humankind's problems. Coincidentally, I changed my career focus from chemistry to medicine as I entered Emory Medical School in September 1971.

I developed an even deeper appreciation of Greenbrier Cove and the surrounding mountains during this time frame. The effects of acid rain caused by sulfur dioxide and nitrous oxides from the burning of fossil fuels were becoming a problem, though I was unaware of the magnitude at the time. The Middle Prong of the Little Pigeon River remained an eternal source of recreation and natural beauty, and I developed a strong affinity to the stream. In addition to tubing, my favorite sport was to find a section of river with a strong current and swim upstream against the raging rapids, like salmon. This activity never failed to rejuvenate me physically and spiritually.

The Middle Prong of the Little Pigeon River is formed by the confluence of more than 100 minor streams draining the slopes of Mt. Le Conte, Mt. Kephart, Mt. Guyot, and Old Black several miles inside the park in Greenbrier Cove. This confluence was the former site of a hotel before it became part of the park. It remains one of the most beautiful spots in the Smokies. When the river swells from heavy rains, kayakers appear out of nowhere to take advantage of the enhanced current for their sport.

These kayakers sparked my imagination for a mythical voyage. This trip would begin at the Porters Creek and Middle Prong junction and continue four miles north until I crossed under U.S. 321 in my kayak or canoe and exited the park. As I continued north, I'd pass Hills Creek Baptist Church, and the covered bridge less than a mile out of the park. After another mile or so, the little town of Pittman Center, founded a century ago by the Methodist Episcopal Church of Philadelphia, Pennsylvania, as a missionary project, would be seen off to my right. Two or three more miles north (downstream), I would pass by Locust Ridge where Dolly Parton's childhood home can be found. I'd continue north to the town of Sevierville, and from there, paddle toward the Douglas Dam, where I would enter the French Broad River that flows west to Knox County. Just outside of Knoxville, the Holston River merging from the north to create the Tennessee River would come into view. I would then see the Clinch, the Little Tennessee, and the Hiwassee Rivers as they emptied into the Tennessee River. As I floated south past Chattanooga and South Pittsburg, and into northern Alabama, I'd pass by Muscle Shoals. I would re-enter Tennessee as I veered north again until I reached Paducah, Kentucky, on the Ohio River. But I'm not finished yet.

I would continue downstream on the Ohio River until it merged with the mighty Mississippi River in Cairo, Illinois. From there I'd start my long journey south passing near Graceland in Memphis; Natchez, Mississippi, and then Baton Rouge, Louisiana. Finally, if I packed enough trail mix, granola bars, and Gatorade and I didn't get run over by a paddleboat or attacked by a hungry alligator, I would arrive at the city of New Orleans. If I could furthermore avoid the attractions of the French Quarter, I'd drift on down through the delta and enter the Gulf of Mexico.

Such a voyage would make my 16-year-old self's five-day canoe trip on the Little Tennessee River seem like child's play. Why would I even contemplate such an unlikely expedition? Even if I let the current do most of the work, it would be an exhausting and, at times harrowing, experience. It seems that water is an integral part of my Personal Legend.

This hypothetical journey is but a reminder of the importance of water travel in the early days of our country. The completion of the Erie Canal in 1825 paved the way for the opening of the Midwest to the Eastern seaboard and was a major facilitator of economic growth. It was soon followed by the development of the railroads and westward expansion.

But my obsession with water is not limited to its use for transportation. The use of water for power generation, agriculture, industry, domestic tasks, recreation, the ecosystem, and as a double agent as both cleaning aid and vehicle for pollutants clearly makes it the most important compound of our existence. It is the essential ingredient of life and makes up about 60 percent of our body by weight. It is no wonder the civilizations that have best utilized their water resources have flourished, while those that existed for too long on outdated water projects are frequently surpassed by those on the forefront of water technology.

The availability of inexpensive, clean water in abundance is easy to take for granted in most of the United States. But in the Western states, cities such as Las Vegas and Los Angeles have had to develop innovative techniques to meet high demand. Some countries, like Australia, have dealt with water shortages more or less successfully with technology such as desalination and recycling. Other countries, such as India, fall far short of American standards. For example, 45 percent of India's population (540 million people) lacks routine access to safe drinking water, and 40 children under age five die each hour from contaminated water. That equates to one death every 90 seconds. Bacteria counts in the Yamuna River frequently exceed 10 million per 100 milliliter (mL). India's standard for safe swimming is 500 per 100 mL. The standard is 250 per 100 mL in our country.

Fortunately, I have never had to struggle with water shortages in either Greenbrier or my primary residence in Concord, North Carolina. The worst I can recall was a restriction on watering our yard about 10 years ago. I know I have been too fascinated with natural water's scenic beauty, mystic properties, and paradoxical personality to worry about its availability in some parts of the world. As Charles Fishman shrewdly notes in *The Big Thirst*, a wonderful treatise on *The Secret Life and Turbulent Future of Water*, it is the duality of water's nature that makes it so fascinating. Water is transparent, but also reflects light. Water is soft and soothing, yet also hard as concrete. Water is comforting, and also threatening. It is both gentle and fierce. Water is the source of life, and a source of death. Water is all-important, indispensable, and almost always free, or essentially free. Water is the most basic necessity to human life, and also a symbol of luxury and indulgence. It is sexy and alluring, while often appalling and repugnant. Water is natural and wild as anything in the world— from whitewater rapids and waterfalls, to the power of hurricanes—and yet water is thoroughly domesticated in everyday life. Water is as familiar as anything in ordinary life, and yet largely ignored, misunderstood, and overlooked.

By 1975, the Age of Aquarius was well underway. Most significantly, the Vietnam War was drawing to an end. After the Vietnamese took the city of Ban Me Thuot on March 10, the dye was cast. On April 30, 1975, the Fall of Saigon, or the liberation of Saigon by the People's Army of Vietnam and the Vietcong, took place, thus ending the 20-year conflict also known as the Second Indochina War. The First Indochina War ended on May 7, 1954, with the French defeat at Dien Bien Phu.

It appears our government misjudged the situation. But peace was at hand. John Kerry, as spokesman for Vietnam Veterans Against the War, could no longer ask: "How do you ask a man to be the last man to die for a mistake?" There was a feeling of humility, but also of hope for the future. A number of important cultural events also occurred in 1975. Sony released their Betamax videocassette recording (VCR) system. The next year, JVC introduced the VHS system, which, by the mid-1980s, had pretty much won the race in video formatting. Perhaps more importantly, Stephen Wozniak and Steve Jobs began working on computer designs. Apple I was released in 1976. Bill Gates and Paul Allen founded Microsoft on April 4, 1975. By this time, the Watergate crisis was resolved and Gerald Ford became our president. It seemed that John Dean, White House Counsel for President Nixon, was telling the truth after all.

I entered Emory Medical School in September 1971 at age 22; I was optimistic on one hand, but also a bit insecure about where this path was headed. I dove into the study of anatomy, microbiology, and pathology, but had no clue how this knowledge would be incorporated and used on a daily basis in a real profession. Furthermore, my expertise in calculus, chemistry, and physics didn't seem to give me any distinct advantage, at least initially. Consequently, I often felt like an outsider desperately searching for a niche. In many ways, I was behind the curve. Many of the students had a richer background in medicine, were worldlier, and more familiar with classic literature than I. This, of course, induced a state of deep humility. At the same time, I resolved to incorporate a few classics into my reading schedule to eventually help remedy that deficiency.

Despite mediocre grades and a lack of direction, I eventually discovered a niche in medicine that utilized my background in chemistry, math, and physics. The specialty of anesthesiology required knowledge of pharmacology and chemistry, and some expertise in math and physics is necessary to understand how drugs are taken up and distributed in the body. The specialty was oriented around the performance of technical procedures and acute care as opposed to one involved with chronic care. Services provided by anesthesiologists were essential to a full-service medical or surgical center, but the intrinsic nature of the specialty was somewhat offbeat compared to a primary care physician. This suited me just fine. I had no preconceived role model in medicine to emulate. I was still trying to pursue my Personal Legend like Santiago by following my intuition. Where would it lead me?

The next spot in my journey was the University of Florida Medical Center in Gainesville. The anesthesia training program there was easily one of the top ten programs in the country. Undoubtedly, the allure of water, beaches, and Disney World exerted a subliminal reinforcement for this decision. In addition, the prospects of living in a mid-sized town was inviting after four years in Atlanta. I had the month of June 1975 off before beginning my residency. This allowed a short visit with my family at Greenbrier, and a brief interlude for reflection. My residency program began July 1, 1975 and ended June 30, 1978. I elected not to do an optional extra year in a subspecialty, such as obstetrical or cardiac anesthesia; at the time, it seemed to be an unnecessary nuance to be certified in a subspecialty. Today, it's all the rage.

Though some months were hectic (such as while serving as a general surgery and cardiovascular surgery intern), on lighter rotations, I found time to read Dostoyevsky, Camus, Maugham, and others, and even play my battered Epiphone acoustic guitar. I also cherished time off for working out, swimming laps, and occasionally visiting Manatee or Blue Spring State Park for the sheer joy of swimming in a freshwater spring. For someone obsessed with a healthy lifestyle, my residency training presented some challenges. I had to eat, sleep, and exercise not on my own schedule, but as my work demands allowed. I can recall doing push-ups at 3 a.m. in the anesthesia call room. I was so busy as a surgery intern that I totally forgot I had stored some potatoes under the sink for future use. When I finally remembered them, they were crawling with maggots and so putrid that I sprayed the whole mess with insecticide and closed the door until I had the energy to deal with it. Another time while on call for anesthesia, I spent the whole night, along with several others, trying to save the life of a young man in a serious vehicular accident. He had suffered severe orthopedic, abdominal, and brain trauma. In a desperate fight to save him, several operations were ongoing simultaneously—an extremely demanding situation for the anesthesia team. Exhausted, I left the hospital around 7:30 a.m., anxiously anticipating the comfort and privacy of my tiny apartment. However, when I turned the key in the ignition to start my car, nothing happened. Not even a chug! With an ominous feeling, I slowly opened the hood to discover the battery was missing. What a cheesy crime! How much could the battery be worth? I wasn't too upset about the cost of a new battery, but why couldn't the thieves be a little more considerate with timing their crime?

By August 1978, I had completed my residency training and moved to Concord, North Carolina with my bride, Heidi, to begin private practice in anesthesia. Heidi, an OR nurse, and I were married in Florida, and would soon start a family. In other words, I began "living the dream," made possible by years of schooling and training. I was clueless as to exactly what "living the dream" would entail, but perhaps that's just as well. We were still in the Age of Aquarius, but it was beginning to have a slightly different feel. Getting up at 5 a.m. routinely, and applying for life insurance and a mortgage, will do that for you. Not to mention the daily challenge of administering anesthetics to patients from one to 92. The Age of Aquarius had no catastrophic ending or dramatic death. We still see glimmers of its existence in an old song, a romantic rant, or a Subaru commercial. But, by 1980, we were clearly entering a new age. The liberals and hippies had their day. See what it got us: political humiliation in Iran, high inflation, and President Jimmy Carter. Never mind these were the results of many long-standing policies and decisions. And Carter's legacy improved by leaps and bounds as we gain historical perspective. At the start of the '80s, people were searching for a way to feel better about themselves and our country.

THE AGE OF REAGAN

Men occasionally stumble over the truth, but most of them pick themselves up and hurry off as if nothing had happened.

—Winston Churchill

Ronald Reagan, our 40th president (1981 – 1989), is frequently credited with ending the Iran Hostage Crisis (1981) and demanding that Mr. Gorbachev "tear down that wall" in 1987. Known as the "Great Communicator," he is also known for his conservative policies of decreased taxation and increased military spending, while advocating an overall decrease in governmental disbursements and regulations.

As a result, his presidency saw a backlash against the environmental activism of the 1970s and a decreased interest in fuel-efficient transportation initiated by the oil embargo of 1973. Big Oil ruled. Perhaps Reagan's boldest move was to appoint James G. Watt as Secretary of the Interior. Watt was accused of decreasing funding for environmental programs, decreasing federal regulatory power, and attempting to eliminate the Land and Water Conservation Fund. He once stated, "We will mine more, drill more, cut more timber."

Ultimately, Watt resigned after enraging the Sierra Club and other environmentalists, in addition to making some racially insensitive remarks. Yet, one poor choice in a cabinet member didn't ruin Reagan's reputation. The problem of ozone depletion and the resulting incidence of skin cancer and effects on the eco-system was largely resolved with the Montreal Protocol, signed in 1987, to ban chlorofluorocarbons (CFCs). Simultaneously, the effects of acid rain were at least being moderated by the environmental acts of the 1970s. Somehow, Reagan got away with playing both sides. His presidency came to a close in 1989 when his VP, George H.W. Bush, succeeded him. Despite undermining much of the civil rights movement and vastly increasing the national debt, Reagan became a hero of the Right. His persona and communication skills were an important ingredient of his success. But what about those "killer trees?"

Yes, in 1981, Reagan made the statement that trees cause more pollution more than cars. Granted, environmental scientists were forced to admit trees do emit terpenes and isoprene compounds that can react with the atmosphere to increase ground level ozone. But this is minor compared to the toxicity of nitrous oxides from cars and other vehicles. What was he thinking? Perhaps a plot for a new movie, *Killer Trees*. I guess every president is allowed at least one gaffe. But to concerned scientists and environmentalists, Reagan's comment was over the top. Shouldn't our leaders be environmentally savvy and knowledgeable about science and math? No biggie.

I wanted some confirmation that the Right highly values these areas of expertise for our current and future welfare. So, I scoured literature for some verification that Reagan supporters revered and incorporated math and science in their political philosophy. Eventually, I found a supporting quote, made years later by George W. Bush, our 43rd president, "Mathematics are one of the fundamentaries [sic] of educationalizing [sic] our youths." Thank goodness! It's reassuring to know our executive branch valued logic and objective reasoning when making important political decisions. It is also confidence-building to know our youths will be *educationalized*.

The Reagan years were good for me personally, despite the unease over environmental issues. Global warming was not yet a major concern, and gas prices were under control. It seemed to be a good time to raise a family. And on November 9, 1989, the Berlin Wall was finally demolished. That had to mean something.

MEDICAL PRACTICE

History teaches us that men and nations behave wisely once they have exhausted all other alternatives.

—Abba Eban

Far and away the most significant activity of my middle years was the private practice of medicine, i.e., anesthesiology in and around Concord, North Carolina. It is a stretch, if not an absurdity, to attempt to describe this endeavor in a few paragraphs. Numbers can't begin to tell the complete story. And yet the story can't be related without the use of numbers. If I were forced to summarize quantitatively, I might say something like this: in more than 39 years of medical practice, I had in excess of 50,000 patient encounters, and directly administered or supervised that many anesthetics. This would include about 50,000 IV starts, more than 35,000 general anesthetics, at least 10,000 epidurals, 5,000 spinal blocks, and several thousand nerve blocks of various types. But it would also include five different hospital CEOs, four changes in the hospital's name, and four different anesthesia groups. On a personal level, it would include the birth of three children, one divorce, one marriage, one malpractice suit, four different primary residences, and serving in numerous positions within the medical society, hospital, anesthesia practice, my local church, and various community activities. I can further claim that I only missed one day of work due to illness. So, if I compared myself to Santiago, it would seem I was well on my way to finding my pot of gold and defining my Personal Legend. But on the other hand, how did these accomplishments mesh with my strong interests in the environmental, a healthy lifestyle, and fascination with water? What did these concerns have to do with my medical practice? Would they become important in later life? Or just become idiosyncratic side interests? Like Peggy Lee, I was asking myself, "Is That All There Is?"

I had no claim to fame other than reaching my destination in good health, devoid of any major political or personal issues. Nevertheless, reaching such a benchmark motivated me to review some of the more noteworthy medical careers from times past. Physicians of antiquity helped set the stage for modern medicine and for me to practice that medicine. For example, Hippocrates (460 – 375 BCE) is considered the father of Western Medicine and was the first to argue that diseases of man were due to natural forces, as opposed to gods or supernatural forces. In other words, medicine was a branch of science enhanced by clinical observations and subject to the laws of cause and effect.

The Persian physician, philosopher, and mathematician, Ibn Sina (980 – 1037), known as Avicenna in the West, was responsible for writing *The Canon of Medicine*. This medical textbook became the most highly regarded work of its kind in Europe and the Islamic world until early modern times. William Harvey (1578 – 1658) was an English physician who studied at both Cambridge and Padua. He is best known for the publication of *On the Motion of the Heart and Blood in Animals* in 1628, and was the first to describe the circulatory system in that blood flowed from the heart in arteries, and after perfusing tissues in the body, returned by the venous system to the heart. This, of course, is so fundamental to the understanding of the basic physiology that we assume it has always been known, but at the time it was a radical concept that refuted the teaching of the Greek physician Galen and other authorities.

In the 19th century, many physicians began to focus on the prevention of infectious diseases. For example, consider the career of Edward Jenner (1749 – 1823). He recognized the connection between cowpox and smallpox and was therefore able to develop the first functional vaccine to control the latter disease. Because of this, smallpox, which once killed 400,000 people a year in Europe alone, was virtually eliminated by the 1970s. Sir Joseph Lister (1827 – 1912) was known as the father of antiseptic surgery. By building on the work of Louis Pasteur, he developed protocols to greatly decrease postoperative infections via techniques to sterilize operative equipment and the surgical field. Likewise, Ignaz Semmelweis, the famous Hungarian obstetrician, also known as the savior of mothers, drastically decreased the incidence of uterine infection after delivery by advocating the simple act of hand washing between procedures. These two physicians dramatically influenced the path of medicine.

Yet perhaps the most revered physician of all is Sir William Osler (1849 – 1912), who received his medical degree from McGill in 1872 and later went on to be a founder of Johns Hopkins University. He is known as the father of modern clinical practice, and for his textbook, *Principles and Practice of Medicine,* 1892. Osler is said to have taken the teaching of medicine out of the classroom and to the bedside. Despite his prolific writing, international fame, and respect by his peers, his foremost desire was to be known as a compassionate teacher of medical students. That he was.

The list of influential physicians is, of course, too long to attempt a credible summary. This brief recap barely scratches the surface. As an anesthesiologist, however, I believe a few more names are worth mentioning. The physician and surgeon Crawford Long (1814 – 1878) is generally credited with successfully administering the first general anesthetic on March 30, 1842, to assist with the removal of a tumor on a patient's neck in his medical practice in Jefferson, Georgia. A hospital in Atlanta was named in his honor and a museum in Jefferson was built to commemorate this historic event. However, the event was not widely publicized nor witnessed by other physicians. As a result, William T.G. Morton, a dentist, is credited with administering the first successful publicly witnessed general anesthetic on October 16, 1846, in the operating theatre of Massachusetts General Hospital for a minor surgical procedure on a patient of surgeon John Collins Warren. Upon successful completion of the procedure, with the patient totally anesthetized he remarked, "Gentlemen, this is no humbug."

For centuries, Humankind had suffered excruciating pain and misery under the surgeon's knife, yet beginning in the 19th century, those days would soon become unpleasant memories. All the above-mentioned physicians were heroes, deserving great praise and recognition, in my opinion. They were crucial to the creation of my specialty.

One anesthesiologist in those early days stands out in my mind as an extraordinary example and role model for all physicians due to his meticulous research and achievements. John Snow was born March 15, 1813 to a working-class family in York, England, the eldest of nine children. He excelled at mathematics and, at age 14, obtained a medical apprenticeship with William Hardcastle near Newcastle-upon-Tyne and later worked as an assistant to a surgeon in various counties. In 1836, Snow allegedly walked 400 miles from Liverpool to London where he enrolled in the Hunterian School of Medicine on Great Windmill Street. He graduated from the University of London in 1844 and was admitted to the Royal College of Physicians in 1850. In 1847, Snow became very interested in anesthesia when he heard about the successful demonstration of general anesthesia in Boston the previous year. He dedicated his time and energy to perfecting the administration of ether and later chloroform. Later in 1847, he published a brief work entitled, *On the Inhalation of the Vapor Ether.* He was the first physician to study the relationship between dosing and patient response and is widely regarded as the first full-time anesthesiologist, administering about 5,000 anesthetics over a 12-year period.

The use of anesthesia for obstetrical pain, however, was controversial. Several leading physicians, along with the Church of England, decided that God intended for women to suffer during childbirth as per biblical verse, "in sorrow thou shalt bring forth children." The issue remained contentious, but on April 7, 1853, at the birth of Prince Leopold, Queen Victoria proclaimed, "We are going to have this baby and we are going to have chloroform." Who else but John Snow was qualified to give her an anesthetic? Four years later, Snow again administered chloroform to the queen on the birth of Princess Beatrice. These events did much to diminish, but not totally eliminate, any opposition to the use of anesthesia for labor and delivery. Becoming the world's foremost anesthesiologist was a major accomplishment, worthy of honor and recognition. Ironically, Snow was ultimately better known for his work in epidemiology.

Snow grew up in a poor section of York near the River Ouse. Due to unsanitary conditions and frequent flooding, waterborne diseases were common. But authorities did not believe diseases were transmitted by water at that time. Later, while living in London in the 1840s, Snow again saw an epidemic of cholera associated with unsanitary conditions and water pollution. In 1849, he published a paper entitled, "On the Mode of Communication of Cholera." He argued that the agent causing the disease of cholera was carried in the water. During the cholera outbreak of 1854 in London, Snow did an extensive review of all cholera cases and plotted their place of origin in relationship to their water supply. With this meticulous methodology, he was able to pinpoint the probable source of the disease to a community well on Broad Street. By removing the handle of the pump to prohibit its use, Snow curtailed the epidemic. Some, however, claimed the epidemic was already dissipating and the handle removal was merely coincidental. By 1866, his theory of cholera transmission was widely accepted. Unfortunately, Snow died prematurely on June 16, 1858, of a massive stroke.

Today, John Snow is known as one of the fathers of epidemiology; a plaque commemorating his legacy as the epidemiologist who resolved the 1854 cholera crisis in London is located on Broad (now Broadwick) Street. The nearby John Snow Pub hosts regular meetings of the John Snow Society. It is somewhat unusual for a physician to gain worldwide fame and be a credit in not just one, but two, seemingly unrelated fields of medicine. The breakthrough accomplishments in both anesthesiology and epidemiology were timely achievements, perhaps both waiting for the right physician to make the critical observations. One might appropriately ask: How are these two achievements related? Did expertise in one specialty facilitate or lend itself to expertise to the other? Or are they both the result of extraordinary genius and totally unrelated? After considerable contemplation, I believe I have unveiled an asset of Snow that was key to both accomplishments. It is simply that he was an astute observer who kept thorough records of his observations. This meticulous methodology allowed him to both perfect the art of anesthesia, and reach logical conclusions about the spread of disease. For some reason, I feel a unique attachment and admiration for John Snow. Certainly, his reputation garnered as an epidemiologist can only embellish the image of anesthesiology as a multi-faceted specialty. Perhaps I can build on this imagery to augment my own career. And, then again, there is the undeniably important role played by water. The miraculous substance that enhances, entertains, intimidates, and supports life at the molecular and spiritual level and sometimes serves as the agent of disease and annihilation.

Certainly, we owe a debt of gratitude to those physicians who made contributions to the art and science of medicine before our time. Our clinical practices today would be quite different without their contributions.

RETIREMENT

The highest reward for a person's toil is not what they get for it, but what they become by it.

—John Ruskin

In my grandparents' day, the concept of retirement was much simpler. You worked 35 years for the railroad, then got your gold watch and quit working. You might have a little garden or occasionally do a small side job, depending on your health, but retiring meant not going to work anymore. For many reasons, that concept has been greatly altered and expanded today. People live much longer. A person born in this country in 1900 could expect to live only about 46 years on the average, while today it's close to 80 years of age. The diversity of available jobs and work schedules has skyrocketed, and many people elect to keep working into old age at a slower pace at the same job, or possibly in a totally different field. Retirement is therefore a process rather than total cessation of employment at a specific time. An employee approaching retirement age frequently has to choose from an array of work options.

When I reached potential retirement age in my early 60s, I received conflicting advice from well-meaning associates and friends. The first group strongly recommended I consider retirement as soon as feasible. Their logic was that I had worked hard and long and now deserved an easier lifestyle so I could spend more time with family and my special interests. I could finally live life as it was meant to be—stress free and full of leisure activities. It made sense. The other group of well-wishers had an opposing view. They suggested if I enjoyed my work, and my employer offered the option of working at a reduced schedule, 30 or so hours a week, why not continue a few more years? They told me I would still have time for family and friends, and a little extra income certainly would be welcome. For that matter, why not work indefinitely as long as you enjoy it, and can cut back on your hours as desired? Isn't work a sustaining and vital part of life? This advice made sense as well.

Of course, job availability and health issues may be critical factors in the retirement process for many. Employees must each decide for themselves how the process will work. For me, the first decisive and objective step in the retirement process began in 2012, when I stopped taking night calls for my group. Although I was still a full-time physician, this move was huge. As an anesthesiologist, I would no longer be paged at all hours of the night to perform a labor epidural, cover an emergency surgery or perform some needed service in the Emergency Department or elsewhere. Thirty-four years of taking calls had been quite a drain on my life and seemed to be a respectable length of servitude. But, psychologically, the process of retirement began much earlier. This would be the time in my career when I felt the bulk of stresses and hurdles were behind me, and I began to focus on the possibilities of an easier life. That time was the summer of 2006, when construction of our mountain home in Emerts Cove was completed.

My wife, Rebecca, and I now had a physical structure around which we could project an idyllic future. Although we had contemplated other possible sites, and even purchased a lot on an upscale golf course near Hendersonville, North Carolina, none of them felt like home. We eventually focused on the Greenbrier area when, in the summer of 2004, we discovered a four-acre tract of land a few hundred yards from the covered bridge on the

Little Pigeon River. At the time we felt unusually lucky to have discovered this little piece of paradise. In retrospect, however, it feels like it was meant to be, almost inevitable. Against the advice of some, we opted for a log home to be built on a fairly steep hillside. Rebecca and I chose a log home plan by Heritage Log Homes and a local builder, Verlis Williams and Sons, to do the construction. They came highly recommended due to their considerable experience with log homes. The first challenge was to create a flat homesite and a sloped driveway from Price Cove Road on the verdant hillside, by the skillful work of a local grader. This enabled us to have easy access and at the same time avoid the appearance of a cliffhanging home. The use of heavy I-beams on the ground floor, and spring-loaded metal rods strategically placed through the 8-inch pine logs, helped stabilize the structure and assure us that this house would be around for years to come.

As construction began, we had an unexpected visit from our closest neighbor, Zenith Whaley. Already well into his 90s, Zenith was a direct descendent of William Whaley and somewhat of a local legend. He was born in Greenbrier Cove in 1914, before it became a national park. In 1934, he was forced to move, along with about a thousand other residents, with the creation of the Smoky Mountains National Park. He married his teenage girlfriend, Maude, in 1936 when she was only 14. Among his accomplishments were serving as pastor of three different primitive Baptist churches, and as a tour guide to many visitors for multiple brief expeditions into the park. The purpose of Zenith's brief visit was to welcome us to the area and give our homesite a blessing. This consisted of about two minutes of chanting and singing to consecrate our land. I couldn't understand what he was saying, but we felt singularly blessed by this colorful character who seemed to project an aura of mysticism. We continued to see him occasionally in the area. Our completed, three-story cabin was nearly 3,000 square feet. The water percolation test on our land only allowed for a two-bedroom home to be constructed.

But we were permitted to have three full bathrooms, and a full basement that could be used as a third bedroom. The top floor had the master bedroom and bath, and a loft that provided a 22-foot tall ceiling for the great room on the main floor. We were pleased with the solid quality of the construction and aesthetics of this log home built on a wooded hillside. The only minor problem for the first several years was the occasional creaking and popping sound of the logs as they contracted. Like other homes in the area, we had our own septic field and water well on opposite ends of the house. Water was found at a depth of over 300 feet, and the well reliably met all our water needs for close to 15 years. On most days, the water flows to the surface freely without the use of a pump, due to adequate pressure of the underground water supply. Named after the wells in Artois, France (Artesium in the Middle Ages), artesian wells are a natural phenomenon and, in some cases, have enough pressure to supply a building of several stories. We consider it a gift. We had the water analyzed by the Sevier County Health Department. They reported the usual minerals and a modest number of coliform bacteria, but no E coli. I have learned not to take clean, reliable water for granted. So far, so good.

The only problem we eventually encountered was with ownership of the property. The deed clearly indicated that Rebecca and I had an unencumbered title to the four acres. But somehow wildlife didn't get the message. Squirrels, bats, snakes, mosquitoes, and carpenter bees, not to mention chickweed, dandelion, buckhorn plantain, crabgrass, and others, continued to act as if they owned the place. The natural environment continued an unrelenting battle to regain control. This established a constant state of warfare with Mother Nature. We engaged in an all-out fight using physical removal, cleaning, spraying, and pest repellants. We closed the space behind the shutters to prevent bats from building homes there. Then we learned the average bat consumes up to 1,000 mosquitoes per hour. So, we decided to let the bats back, but by that time, they had written us off as ungrateful hosts and were seeking alternate housing arrangements. All this conflict begs the question: who really owns the land?

For several thousand years, the Cherokee Indians roamed the Smoky Mountains for hunting, fishing, and foraging. Later, they grew corn, beans, and squash. For about 225 years now, property owners in the state of Tennessee have claimed the land as their own. This is an infinitesimal time span in the overall scheme of things. My wife and I legally own the land. But it may be that Mother Nature holds the trump card. In the years since 2006, we made frequent trips to our mountain home to become more familiar with our new neighbors and environs. Price Cove Road was a dead-end road beginning near the river and running about a half-mile up the cove. At the end of the road were the homes of six families who were all closely related members of the extended Price family. We got to know Buford Price and Loy Price and their families fairly well. We also met the Hendricks just down the road from us, and Kathy Daily, who lived directly below us and owned the larger parcel of land from which our four acres were carved out. In addition, we met several members of the Huskey clan, who lived in Emerts Cove close to the river, and eventually members of the Ogle family, who lived nearby and played a major role historically in the commercial growth of the Gatlinburg area. At the same time, we reacquainted ourselves with Greenbrier Cove and the park as a whole. As I had visited this area annually since age five, I was already quite familiar with the river and a number of trails. But that was from the perspective of a tourist or visitor. Now we were acquainted as locals. We discovered new trails a little off the beaten path, shortcuts, and features of the mountains most tourists didn't notice.

I was vaguely aware of the park's history during my visits in earlier years. I viewed the Greenbrier Cove as a beautiful section of the national park that just happened to contain homesites of early settlers. Now I tend to view the area as the former homesite of multiple families that just happened to have been turned into a national park. Evidence of old homesteads exists everywhere. There are several abandoned homesites, rock walls, old roadbeds, and a few remaining chestnut fence posts. At one time, the cove harbored 23 gristmills, four schools, four grocery stores, and a hotel. It is fascinating to discover remaining stone structures and attempt to figure out their original use. Also, within the cove are 17 cemeteries, three of which were for Native Americans. Greenbrier Cove may therefore fit the definition of a true-to-life history museum. Those who look with a discerning eye can discover so much treasure. Trials and tribulations of the early settlers and indigenous peoples are imbedded in these hills.

A year or so after building our cabin, we learned Zenith wanted to show Rebecca and me some Indian artifacts in the park. We jumped at the chance. After driving about two miles into the park with Zenith and our real estate agent, Susan, we parked our car on the side of the road. We carefully followed Zenith as he led us over uneven, rocky ground and through thick brush until we approached the riverbed. Here, a 15- to 20-foot shelf of smooth gray river rock bordered the river. Zenith pointed out several circular smooth indentations in the rock that effectively created a natural bowl shape. These were used more than 200 years ago by the Cherokee to grind corn for consumption. Had this piece of information come from anyone other than Zenith, I might have questioned its veracity, but Zenith's word was indisputable. I tried to imagine thinly clad Cherokee ardently grinding corn with a wooden pole by the river's edge. Then I thought how easy it was for us to walk into a grocery store and purchase a sack of flour or corn meal. Our separation from Mother Nature sometimes seems to hinder our appreciation of how our culture evolved. Unfortunately, Zenith died in May 2010, a month before his 96th birthday. He was survived by his wife of 74 years, Maude, five children, eight grandchildren, 16 great-grandchildren, and four great-great-grandchildren. But, equally important, he left a priceless legacy of history, folklore, and love of the mountains.

The first few years after our cabin was built were also blessed with the occasional visit of another neighbor. Ursus americanus, or the American black bear, is indigenous to the Smoky Mountains. Out of an estimated 400,000 in the continental United States, about 1,500 live in the Great Smoky Mountains National Park. In my pre-cabin years, I was quite aware that bears lived in the area and I had seen a quite a few. But in the 60-plus years I've vacationed in the Greenbrier area, I never saw one in or around the Little Pigeon River where we swam, innertubed, and spent the night. So, you can imagine my surprise when we discovered a significant number of black bears were roaming the hills just several hundred yards up Price Cove Road near the cabin.

Our first such furry visitor arrived after Rebecca baked some blueberry muffins. The bear cub promptly showed up on the hillside behind the cabin to take his share. Later, one actually climbed down the steep hill and made it onto the back patio, just a few feet from the sliding glass door. Yet another time, we spotted a yearling wandering aimlessly around the side yard and behaving bizarrely. Regrettably, we found his body lying in the middle of the road the next morning. The unfortunate cub had been prowling around someone's garage and received a bullet in his head. It's too bad—he was probably just looking for a honey jar. Sadly, I pulled his body off the road to the shoulder. He really did seem like a big teddy bear.

Since the park has about 10 million visitors per year, bear-tourist interactions are fairly common. But serious injuries are extremely rare. Only one known fatality was documented in the last 50 years and that was in the Elkmont area, in 2000. Another possible case occurred about 35 years ago. The body of a person missing for a week was found mauled by bears. It was believed, however, that the mauling probably occurred after his death rather than being the cause. Black bears are omnivores and eat a wide variety of foods. Their favorites are grasses, berries, roots, and insects. They will, however, eat fish and small mammals, and feed on carrion. Males may weigh as much as 600 pounds, while females are rarely over 180 pounds. We have a picture of a bear on our refrigerator estimated to weigh about 400 pounds. Our neighbor, less than a quarter mile away, snapped this photo while the bear explored his yard.

Bears can run up to 30 mph and are very good climbers. So, if you meet one in the wild, don't try to run away. Just stop any aggressive motion and move away slowly and sideways, so you can keep an eye on him. An unprovoked attack is extremely unlikely. It is illegal to approach a bear within 50 yards. A close approach might be interpreted as an aggressive move. Bears actually do have good vision as well as an excellent sense of smell. But, just like humans, they may occasionally be oblivious to their surroundings. They can be unpredictable and moody at times. But they aren't always grumpy. Nevertheless, it makes sense to give them their space. I am intrigued by these adorable animals. There is, however, no reason to avoid hiking in the Smokies for fear of Ursus americanus. All that's needed is common sense and respect.

These pre-retirement years in the mountains were conducive to relaxing and helped me ease into full retirement. They also gave me ample time to contemplate what further projects or ideologies I might pursue in the future. During this timeframe, there were two important experiences in the Greenbrier area that critically influenced my mindset, although I didn't appreciate their significance at the time. The first occurred in 2012, during a brief visit in the fall. We learned about two trails beginning in Greenbrier Cove, a little under the radar for most tourists. There was the Rhododendron Creek Trail starting right off Greenbrier Road in the park. This trail offered multiple spectacular views of cascading water. We have hiked it multiple times. But there also was the scenic and interesting Injun Creek Trail, beginning near the ranger station off Greenbrier Road about one mile into the park. The hike was a roughly 3.4-mile (6.8 roundtrip) excursion that led to a very interesting historical artifact.

Allegedly, a once fully functional steam engine was partially submerged in the creek bed since 1920. Rebecca and I decided to see for ourselves. We started mid-morning with our hiking sticks, and a daypack with water and ham sandwiches. The hike was pleasant enough and the seasonal colors created a visual wonderland. However, nothing quite prepared us for the ultimate shocking vista. Without warning, we came upon what looked like a real train wreck. A steam engine smokestack, boiler, wheels, and various gears were strewn over a shallow segment of Injun Creek. Of course, some metal parts were partially buried and most were covered with moss, but their form and historic functions were easy to identify. The only confusing feature was the size of the individual components. Their dimensions seemed to be about half that of a normal-sized steam locomotive. Yes, this wreck was from a steam engine, but not one from a train.

In 1920, one of Ike Huskey's sons was operating their multi-purposed Nichols-Shepard traction engine on their farmland when he got too close to the creek bank. It toppled over and landed in the creek bed where it has sat ever since. The steam engine tractor for agricultural uses was introduced around 1868. Their heyday in this country was the late 1800s – early 1900s. Some were still used here in the 1930s, and in the UK in the 1950s. These machines augmented farmers' abilities to transport goods and do routine farm work such as plowing. Ironically, workhorses sometimes pulled them to the field to perform their duties. I suspect the Huskey's traction machine that wrecked in 1920 was one of the last in the area. Gas-powered combustion engines were the way of the future. A typical efficiency rating for a steam engine's heat-to-mechanical energy was about six percent. For the internal combustion-engine, it was roughly 36 percent at the time.

The first successful atmospheric steam engine was built in 1712 by Thomas Newcomen as a means to pump water out of ever-increasingly deep coal mines. Although almost 100 were in use by 1734 in England, they had many drawbacks. They were very cumbersome and used a prodigious amount of coal for fuel, with an energy efficiency rating of only about 0.7 percent. James Watt of Glasgow (no relation to Reagan's secretary of energy) made dramatic improvements to the engine design by creating a separate condenser for the steam, thereby quadrupling the energy output of the Newcomen engine.

An efficient steam engine had two very important functions. It could pump water out of the coal mine to better increase output from the mine. It could also be used to power bellows for iron furnaces. Watts' engine was patented in 1769 and was commercially available in 1776. Steam power was therefore synergistic with coal mining and iron production, which increased twenty-fold between 1788 and 1839. The use of waterwheel energy continued alongside steam power.

In the 1830s, the hydraulic turbine further augmented the power generated by falling water. By the mid-19th century, however, steam power became decidedly superior. In addition, although heavy and cumbersome by today's standards, steam engines were portable and therefore more adaptable to multiple tasks. With improvements in efficiency and their mass-to-energy ratio, steam engines were incorporated into factories for textiles and iron production.

The first uses of steam power for transportation were on waterways. In England, Patrick Miller's *Charlotte Dundas* in 1802, and in the U.S., Robert Fulton's *Clermont* in 1807, were the first steam-powered boats. The first Atlantic crossing was from Quebec to London in 1833 by the *Royal William*. Railroads soon followed steamboats; the first commercial railroad was between Liverpool and Manchester England in 1830. Railroads came into being in this country with the first transcontinental line, completed in 1869. However, steam engines were not as useful off rails due to their great mass and the lack of good roads in the 19th century. It's interesting to note that steam engines continued to play an important role through WW II. The dominant U.S. cargo carriers, Liberty Ships (EC2), were powered by a three-cylinder steam engine with an oil-fired furnace. In Alaska from 1942 to 1946, a number of steam engines had a vital role in our defense strategy against a possible Japanese attack. They were used to bring supplies on the White Pass & Yukon Route (formerly used during the Alaskan Gold Rush), to the city of Whitehorse for the construction of the Alaska Highway. These steam locomotives were built by the Baldwin Locomotive Works in Philadelphia, Pennsylvania, in the late 1930s and early 1940s. In 1943, they carried 281,962 tons of freight for the war effort. Some of these narrow-gauge locomotives wound up at Tweetsie Railroad, founded in 1957 near Blowing Rock, North Carolina, and later in East Tennessee for the creation of Rebel Railroad in 1961. The latter changed hands and in 1986 became Dollywood, co-owned by Herschend Family Entertainment and entertainer Dolly Parton.

It seems easy to find undeniable evidence of the glory days of steam engines. The steam engine lying in Injun Creek is about 10 miles from the steam locomotives in Dollywood. Steam engines were the inanimate prime movers of industry of the 19th and early-20th centuries. But they did have some drawbacks. One ride on the Dollywood Express will make this obvious. The smoke and soot billowing from the smokestack are impressive, yet annoying, to say the least. Most people believe the increase in atmospheric CO_2—which began in the late 19th century and continued to present times—was initially the result of burning coal for steam power and other uses. But steam engines had other concerns.

On December 27, 1934, Thomas W. Craft, a 22-year-old, boarded the miners' work train in Montgomery, West Virginia around 6 a.m. for the 12-mile commute up the mountain to the Elkhorn Piney Coal Mining Company. The train consisted of four coaches pulled by a steam engine locomotive hooked up in reverse, so the engine backed up the mountain. As the train pulled out of the tiny town of McDunn, a mile from the top, the boiler exploded without warning. Several men sitting in the closest coach car were decapitated. Many others were scalded and mangled. A part of the boiler flew off and crashed into a house, barely missing two young children in their bedroom. It was a chaotic nightmare. Eighteen men, including Thomas W. Craft, died on the first day; about 20 seriously injured miners were taken to Coal Valley Hospital in Montgomery, where bedlam prevailed. It was so crowded that doctors were hampered in performing their duties. Mrs. Leona Scott Craft was devastated by the tragic death of her new husband. Fortunately for me, however, she eventually remarried and had three children with her second husband, Donald Baird: Thane Scott, Rebecca Ellen and Lissa Ann. My wife, Rebecca, would never have been conceived had the train catastrophe not happened.

With full retirement drawing closer, my professional corporation, Northeast Anesthesia and Pain Specialists (NAPS), sponsored a retirement pool party at a partner's home for my colleague Scott Aumuller and me. Scott was likewise anticipating a life away from work. This was September 2015. As seems to occasionally happen, I was the only one to actually get in the pool. I continued to work at a reduced level through December 2017. However, the event officially labeled me as a has-been, someone with one foot on Easy Street. I sort of liked the feeling. As I implied earlier, there were two major experiences in my last work years that influenced my state of mind. The first one concerned steam engines. The second one was much more dramatic. It occurred in November 2016.

Gatlinburg Fires 2016

Fire is a good servant, but a bad master.

—*Proverb*

On November 28, 2016, a complex of fires raged in and around Gatlinburg, either due to wind-driven embers or downed power lines. The fires spread to the surrounding area and, by December 9, had burned more than 17,000 acres, destroyed over 2,400 buildings and resulted in 14 fatalities. Total damage was estimated at 500 million dollars. It was one of the worst disasters in history for Tennessee, and the worst fire in the eastern U.S. since the 1947 fire in Maine that killed 16 people. The exact cause of the fire was controversial. November weather was very dry with a humidity reading as low as 17 percent on November 27th. Wind speeds as high as 87 mph (hurricane force) were recorded. There was plenty of fuel available in the form of dried leaves and branches. Thus, conditions were ideal for a major conflagration. Of note, however, a hiker captured two teenagers hiking on the nearby Chimney Tops trail on November 23rd with his GoPro camera. They possessed matches. Smoke was evident in the background and the Chimney Top fire had begun around this time. Officials elected to allow the fire to burn. No one anticipated the nearly 90 mph freak winds that would develop five days later.

When these pictures were revealed to officials, the teenagers, aged 15 and 17, were arrested and charged with aggravated arson. Understandably, the locals were furious and some demanded they be tried as adults. This was serious business. On the surface, the case against the teens seemed like a slam dunk. The trial was ongoing. Yet on June 30, 2017, defense attorney Gregory P. Isaacs held a news conference in nearby Knoxville, Tennessee. The arson charges were dropped because the state could not reasonably prove a direct causal relationship between the boys' horseplay with matches and the devastating fires. Analysis of the fire path by photos and eyewitnesses failed to prove the prosecution's case. In addition, some witnessed that power lines downed by winds were also causing fires. As a clincher, the state authorities had to admit they didn't actually have the authority to prosecute a possible crime committed on federal territory (the park). It seems there had been a rush to judgment.

Our cabin is about six miles east of Gatlinburg, so obviously we were quite concerned when we heard reports of the fire. Calling from our North Carolina home on November 29th, our mountain neighbors assured us that the flames had not reached our home in Emerts Cove. They could, however, see fires a mile or so away toward Gatlinburg. We were very relieved. A physician friend and his family were not so lucky. Their mountain home, somewhat closer to town, completely burned down. Two weeks or so later, Rebecca and I were able to inspect our cabin. Our mountain home and everything in the immediate area were totally untouched by the flames. A few miles closer to town, the damage was impressive but sporadic. The Little House of Pancakes was totally untouched, yet, a few hundred yards to the east, the Mountain View Restaurant was destroyed. This same scenario repeated throughout the Gatlinburg area. Patches of total destruction were interspersed with buildings that appeared unscathed. The main strip in downtown Gatlinburg showed little evidence of a conflagration, while parallel streets both to the north and the south side incurred heavy damage. These findings confirmed the theory that either the complex of fires had multiple points of origin, or the extraordinarily strong winds were responsible for their broad spread. More likely both factors were relevant.

Although the Greenbrier and Emerts Cove areas were spared, the Cobbly Nob Community a few miles east suffered heavy damage. The loss of life and property was devastating to the local community. But, fortunately, there was some good news. Dolly Parton, a native of the community, initiated a charity, My People Fund, which raised over eight million dollars. She personally contributed at least three million. This fund enabled all affected families to receive a thousand dollars per month for at least five months. In many ways, the mountain community was drawn together. The fires, known officially as the 2016 Great Smoky Mountain wildfires, left us feeling perplexed. We knew such vicious fires had occurred elsewhere, like in the Southwestern U.S., and in developing countries, but not in East Tennessee. It was comparable to a hurricane moving 200 miles inland to strike the city of Charlotte (Hugo, 1989) or a superstorm dropping 32 inches of snow on Mount Le Conte in October (Sandy, 2012). It wasn't supposed to happen. We all scratched our heads.

As a chemistry major, I knew a little more about fire than the average person. Fire is a chemical reaction between oxygen and biomass which releases heat, light, and usually smoke. In a sense it is the opposite of photosynthesis, in which plants are synthesized with the help of sunlight. There are three elements needed to create fire: fuel, oxygen, and an ignition source. Two out of three won't do. I also knew fire had played an important role in the evolution of Humankind for cooking and metallurgy, and also for religion and philosophy. At one time, early Greek philosophers thought the entire world was made of earth, water, fire, and air.

According to Greek mythology, Prometheus stole fire from Zeus to benefit mortals. Other cultures had similar myths about fire. Furthermore, I had heard the terms "good fire" and "bad fire," but I had not spent a huge amount of time contemplating the fire phenomenon. Like water, fire was ubiquitous, vital for life, and taken for granted. I elected to consult a renowned expert on the subject. Stephen J. Pyne, emeritus professor at Arizona State University, is one of the top fire scholars in the world, if not guru-in-chief. His most recent publication, *Fire Second Edition*, came highly recommended and I learned a good bit by reading this text.

Sometime around 420 million years ago, the right combination of fuel, oxygen, and heat occurred to sustain burning. Before this time burning did not exist. Man's adoption of fire about a million years ago was arguably his most profound contribution to the advancement of civilization. It's impossible to discuss the advancement of man without discussing fire—whether referring to agriculture, warfare, industrial development, or ecology in general. The first naturally occurring fires were in all probability caused by lightning strikes. In the Southwest, lightning causes roughly 2,000 fires a year. Whether a fire burns out or spreads widely depends mostly on the availability of fuels and the geographic features of the landscape. At some point hominins (early man) learned how to capture and control fire. By using flames to cook meats and plants, he greatly decreased the possibility of ingesting toxins and parasites and made digestion easier. Cooking with fire, therefore, is believed to have assisted early man in developing bigger brains and smaller guts. Cooking became the emblem of domesticated fire. As Man tamed fire to clear fields for planting, natural fires and domesticated fires co-existed. While this may have been bad for some, it became obvious that organisms can live with fire, some thrive with it, and others can't live without it.

At various times, societies have attempted to totally eradicate natural fires and, when that occurs, vegetation tends to overgrow and create excessive fuel. When a fire eventually does occur, the resulting one will be far worse than if the natural fire had not been extinguished. Ironically, attempting to eradicate all fires leads to worse fires. It is no more unnatural to have a world with fire than to have a world without fire.

The history of cities is frequently a tale of how citizens have dealt with fires. The first fire codes can be traced to the Code of Hammurabi from 1776 BC in Babylon. But each city has a unique fire history. The Great Fire of London in 1666 was aided by a dry east wind that swept the city, instead of the usual moist winds from the Atlantic Ocean. The Great Chicago Fire of 1871 was largely due to very dry shifting and gusty winds in the region. In 1906, the San Francisco fire that followed the earthquake was only controlled when the winds abated.

Fire as a weapon is well engrained in our history and lexicon. The term "fire and sword" is self-explanatory. The invention of gunpowder by the Chinese in the 9th century AD gave added meaning to the command, "Fire!" In fact, modern warfare's use of incendiary bombs is much more effective than purely explosive ones. The air attacks on Japan in WW 11 wreaked havoc mostly by fire damage. Even the atomic bombs dropped on Hiroshima and Nagasaki in 1945, caused more damage from secondary fires than the initial explosion. Recently, engines, cartridges, and rockets have replaced open flames. Likewise, the Gulf War (August 2, 1990—February 28, 1991) was culminated with burning oil fields.

In modern cities today, open fires are vanishing. The fireplace in most homes is purely decorative or a token to the past. The Industrial Revolution depended on controlling fossil fuels, so more and more were petroleum based, in refined combustion chambers with controlled movement of fuel, heat, and air. Burning still took place but was not visible. Today's technology has separated the point where combustion takes place and resulting effects of energy are observed. Risk of fire is somewhat less, but potential for an extensive fire is still present.

Whether natural, agricultural, or industrial, all fires have something in common. They release carbon dioxide, methane, and other greenhouse gases into the atmosphere. Increasingly, greenhouse gases are coming from East Asia but, with hydraulic fracturing (fracking), even our country is extracting more fossil fuels. The carbon dioxide molecule released from industrial activity in this country is no different from one release from charcoal burning or land clearing in Indonesia. Industrial fires are unlike natural fires in that they don't depend on the climate and geography for initiation. But, more and more, they add greenhouse gases to the atmosphere, along with other fires that may potentially affect the climate's future.

Increasingly, many parts of the world are gaining new economic, military, and political power from new sources of combustion. Societies are not eager to give this up. With Prometheus unbound, the challenge will be to restrain him.

Certainly, the megafire that spread through Gatlinburg in 2016 was devastating. What could be done to avoid a repeat conflagration? Communication problems may have contributed, but the abundance of fuel and the unexpected extreme winds seemed to set the stage. After three years, the city appears pretty much normal and only a local could point out where buildings were destroyed. The burned areas in the woods are largely disguised by new growth vegetation; in a few places, however, the trees still display their blackened scars.

So, in the last few years before full retirement, two unique experiences created lasting memories: the visual of a steam engine wreck from a century ago, and the aftermath of the more recent horrific inferno in the Smokies near our mountain home. These two phenomena were not related in any obvious manner. They seemed to be random and unexpected events that occurred in our universe and, yet, somehow, they trigged activity somewhere in my brain. The growth of power from steam engines greatly motivated the economics of mining and burning coal starting in the 19th century. This was compounded by the rapid increase of burning petroleum products to power the internal combustion engine. Most scientists believe the resulting increase in atmospheric CO_2 along with other combustion byproducts have contributed to the modest degree of surface temperature increase being documented. At the same time, many believe that the incidence of fires is being enhanced by this increase. Of course, I am not suggesting a causal relationship between these two events. Nor do I argue against many other thermal influences at play. But it seemed these experiences were symbolic of an evolving universe. Were there mystical forces at work behind the scenes to make such a display? It may be unjustified to connect the dots, but as a result of these anomalies coinciding near the time of my retirement, I developed a keener interest in the interaction of human activity and the environment. Were humans making the earth warmer? I began reading books about climate change from both sides of the debate. It seems the issue has been highly polarized and emotionalized by zealots on either side. Likewise, I read a number of books on the importance of water to civilization and the environment. I might still be a hopeless romantic trying to discover his Personal Legend, but at least I would be a well-informed one. I could only hope the "whole universe would conspire to help me to find it," as it did with Santiago.

THE PITTMAN
COMMUNITY CENTER

A man must consider what a rich realm he abdicates when
he becomes a conformist.

— *Publius Syrus*

The history of Pittman Center holds a treasure trove of stories reflecting the colorful mountain culture in the area. Located just two and a half miles north of the Greenbrier entrance to the Great Smoky Mountains Park, this narrative greatly overlaps and complements the history of the settlements and migrations of the mountain people in the Greenbrier Cove. Reviewing the fascinating history of Pittman Center greatly enhances learning the ways of mountain people. In May 2000, the National Trust for Historic Preservation designated Pittman Center as one of the "Dozen Distinctive Destinations" in the U.S., ranking it number two out of 12. Unlike the Greenbrier Cove settlements initiated by William Whaley and family in 1810, the Pittman Community Center began as a mission project of the Methodist Episcopal Church.

The mission's inspiration came from Reverend Dr. John Sevier Burnett, a native of Jackson County, North Carolina. After serving a number of mountain communities in Western North Carolina and East Tennessee, he became obsessed with the dream of creating a much-needed school to make Christian education available for kids in remote mountain areas. In the summer of 1919, while visiting families in the Greenbrier area, he discovered a beautiful wooded area near the junction of Webb Creek and the Middle Prong of the Little Pigeon River. He felt divinely inspired to create his dream mission at that site. All he had to do was obtain the financial backing. In 1919, the Annual Centenary Conference of the Methodist Church was held in Columbus, Ohio. There, Dr. Burnett requested the approval and financial support of the Board of Home Missions of the Methodist Church. In this effort, he received assistance from his good friend, Dr. Eli Pittman, the presiding elder of the Elmira district in New York. Together they secured funding to purchase 1,500 acres to develop a campus for educational and health services. The joyful news spread throughout the mountain communities. Local loggers, carpenters, and craftsmen of various types volunteered from the workforce. In addition to felling and transporting trees to various sawmills, hundreds of boulders, river rocks, and loads of sand were transported from the river to the construction site by teams of horses and dedicated mountain men.

Dr. Burnett also insisted on cutting adequate quantities of lumber to make barns for raising cattle, a woodworking shop to employ locals to make furniture, and eventually a cannery. The campus would not only be a center for education, but also a community center in the full sense of the word. Although many locals insisted the new campus should be called the Burnett Community Center for the doctor's vital role in inspiring and supervising the facility's construction, Dr. Burnett preferred to have it named in honor of his good friend, Dr. Eli Pittman.

One hundred fifty students from grades one to 12 attended the opening day of school on August 15, 1921. The school boasted an amply sized auditorium and six well-ventilated classrooms, along with a training room, domestic kitchen, and sewing rooms in the basement. It had electric lighting, steam heat, a water system with toilets in the basement, and showers and baths for the teachers. The water needs were met by spring water diverted from Sol Hollow to large storage tanks just above the center. To help dedicate the opening of the school, Dr. Burnett planned a three-day celebration. On September 7, 1921, the local paper noted, "The Pittman Community School at Emerts Cove will be dedicated Sunday, September 18th, Monday, September 19th, and Tuesday, September 20th. This school is worthwhile and the public is cordially invited to attend the dedicatory exercises." The addresses and sermons were given by Bishop Frank Bristol of the Holston Conference, Doctors of Divinity Paul Vogt of Philadelphia and Frank Stapleton, District Superintendent, and Dr. William Barnett from the University of Tennessee (UT). The final day was honored by the presence of Congressman Carroll Reece, Hon. J.B. Brown, and Governor Alfred A. (Alf) Taylor. Even the Guard of Honor of a hundred horsemen and brass band from UT were on hand to accompany the governor.

The Pittman Center School continued to grow under Dr. Burnett's direction and later under the leadership of Dr. Luther Flynn. However, transportation was a major problem. The road conditions were deplorable and horse-drawn wagons were the best option. Sevier County had a policy of requiring all able-bodied men to work the roads six days a year or pay an assessment of nine dollars to the county treasurer. By 1929, three trucks and three wagons were available for transportation. In the 1930s, the local CCC and the Work Projects Administration (WPA) in Greenbrier Cove built bridges, and sufficiently improved roads to allow school buses to run.

As the school grew, buildings were added to accommodate athletics, crafts, and home economics. The curriculum was expanded to include classes in plumbing, auto mechanics, and printing, among others. In addition, the Center provided employment for locals with its business ventures in a 4,000-tree orchard, a nursery, and in craft programs including weaving, basketry, and woodworking. These ventures provided a critical source of income for many families during the Great Depression.

By 1947, the Pittman Community Center payroll expanded to 31 workers and the center gained notoriety for its accomplishments. In 1948, nearly 200 visitors came from India, China, Belgian Congo, British West Indies, Czechoslovakia, Nigeria, Belgium, Cuba, France, and half the states in the Union. By the early 1960s, however, maintenance and repair costs of the Pittman School, as well as the Phi Beta Phi High School in Gatlinburg, were becoming excessive. The Sevier County Board of Education wisely opted to consolidate the two schools. In 1963, the new Gatlinburg-Pittman High School opened between the two towns on a ridge with a good view of Mt. Le Conte. For a number of years, grades one to eight remained at the old location but eventually were moved as well.

The Mission Board decided in 1964 that Dr. Burnett's dream had been realized. They decided money could now be better spent elsewhere. In July 1974, the Town of Pittman Center was chartered. The home economics building and acreage were purchased in 1976 and used as a Town Hall that houses the police station and senior citizens center. Most of the original buildings of the Pittman Center School and Community are gone; of the original 1,500 acres, about 400 were condemned by the State of Tennessee to build the Foothills Parkway in the 1970s. Much of the rest sold to developers around 2000. Also gone are the annual fairs with craft exhibits, athletic competition, mountain music, and revivals. In 1993, however, the mayor of Pittman Center, Judy Perryman, instituted "Heritage Day." This one-day annual event occurs the third Saturday in September to help re-create the atmosphere of the past with drama, music, games, competition, food, and crafts.

Perhaps the most fascinating aspect of the Pittman Community Center story has to do with its professional medical care. When the school opened in 1921, there were no hospitals in all of Sevier

County, and very few doctors. To help remedy this problem, the Board of Missions decided to recruit a full-time physician to serve the area with the financial assistance of Francis E. Baldwin, president of the Thatcher Manufacturing Company. Mr. Baldwin offered to build a fully equipped medical clinic and provide a monthly salary of $125 for the physician director. By happenstance, Dr. Pittman heard about an interesting physician who had just completed his medical training and internship at Binghamton City Hospital in Binghamton, New York.

Dr. Robert F. Thomas was born on June 21, 1891, to a poor family in Scranton, Pennsylvania. His family somehow managed to send him to Syracuse University in Syracuse, New York, where he eventually qualified to be a missionary minister. After serving as a missionary for three years in Penang, Malaya (Malaysia) where he headed a school of 1,400 boys and preached to the English-speaking residents, he realized he could be a more effective missionary if he also had medical training. Returning to the U.S. in 1919, he received his medical degree from his alma mater in 1925, and completed his internship at Binghamton City Hospital in Binghamton, New York a year later. While attending medical school, he earned $100 per year by serving as pastor for two rural churches. His plans to return to Malaya as a missionary in 1926, however, were thwarted by his wife's poor health.

The position offered Dr. Thomas by the Methodist Mission Board to serve the poor mountain people of Tennessee was therefore accepted with great enthusiasm. The first part of the journey from New York to Tennessee went just fine. Dr. Burnett warned Dr. Thomas about the terrible roads and difficulty in getting around. But Thomas had no idea it would take eight hours to drive the last 25 miles of the trip between Newport and Pittman Community Center, with his wife, four-year-old son, and all their belongings packed in the family's Chevy. Traversing swollen streams on log bridges, muddy trails with hairpin turns, and steep slippery slopes, Thomas was certain that the shifting furniture would upend the car, or a broken axle might do them in. Upon finally reaching the newly built Baldwin Clinic, the Thomas family had no choice but to share the building with two women while their house was being built.

But who could have prepared Thomas on how to deal with the mountain people and their superstitions? Grannies still delivered babies and treated illnesses. Occasionally, they would put a pan of cold water under a child with typhoid to cure his fever. Sometimes the husband of a woman in labor would place an axe under her bed to "cut" the pain. Eventually, Thomas traveled many miles on horseback to make house calls and see clinic visitors. Besides providing medical services, he also routinely preached at two local churches and performed weddings and funerals. Slowly, he gained the trust and admiration of the mountaineers.

Around 1948, a younger physician was interested in following Dr. Thomas for a few days to see if he might want to join the practice. Two out of the four nights, they went out after midnight for house calls. In the pitch-blackness, they had to cross a shaky swinging bridge and walk through cow pastures and pig pens to treat a youngster on the brink of death. Afterward, the visiting physician sent a letter thanking Dr. Thomas for the experience of seeing a world he never knew existed. He declined an offer to join, claiming, "The work you do is most challenging, but it is too hard for me." In 1942, Dr. Thomas was appointed the superintendent of Pittman Community Center in addition to his other duties. Under his guidance, they acquired a dependable outside source of electricity from TVA in 1947, and three telephones from Bell in 1949. Pittman Community Center was designated as a fourth-class post office and Dr. Thomas also accepted the position of postmaster with a monthly salary of $8.33. In 1955, he facilitated the sale of the school to the Sevier County Board of Education but continued as superintendent until he retired in 1964.

Several vignettes help illustrate why Dr. Thomas was so

respected and eventually became a living legend. He received a modest stipend from the Board of Missions but generally got paid by whatever means a patient could afford, including food, firewood, chickens, and produce. One woman insisted on paying for a delivery years afterward because, as she said, "Doc, I don't believe my old man is ever going to get around to paying you." With that she set a small sack of coins on his desk and asked him, "Is that enough?" Dr. Thomas did a quick search of the record and told her the bill was paid in full.

In January 1946, he had to ride his horse a few miles north to Locust Ridge where he delivered the fourth child of a poor family. The husband gave him a sack of cornmeal, and the wife would eventually have eight more babies. But the fourth one was different. She developed a love and proficiency of country and gospel music and began writing and performing music at an early age. I personally recall seeing her perform on a local TV show in Knoxville. Eventually, Dolly Rebecca Parton would become one of the wealthiest, most successful female performers of all time.

In December 1947, Thomas was gifted a Jeep by a church in Pennsylvania, making his horseback riding no longer necessary. The peripatetic physician soon became known as the "Jeep Angel." Although officially retired in 1964, he continued to perform many duties, including preaching stints, weddings, funerals, and giving talks at various clubs, organizations, and graduations. He completed his earthly mission on June 4, 1980, just shy of his 89th birthday. His obituary statements referred to him as:

"A True Shepherd"

"The Albert Schweitzer of the Smokies"

"The Real Man"

"A Man Whose Shoes Cannot Be Filled"

I regret that I never had the opportunity to meet Dr. Thomas. When he died, I was in my early years of medical practice in North Carolina. It's too bad—his exemplary career is a worthy guidepost for any physician seeking his Personal Legend.

The Elephant in the Room

*It is not easy to find happiness in ourselves, and it is
impossible to find it elsewhere.*

—Agnes Repplier

As I celebrated my early retirement years, I noticed some
subtle changes in myself. Not so much in my slowly declining
physical status, but in how I viewed people and the world in
general. Instead of pretending everyone was more or less a permanent physical fixture on our planet, I began to view individuals as transient creatures with a finite existence. Their soul, or
metaphysical footprint, may endure, but otherwise they are just
visitors on earth marking time. It's almost like I was looking
down from a futuristic vantage point. This disturbing, somewhat
anti-social point of view was not necessarily moribund or driven
by paranoia or personal angst. Nor was it motivated by a
venomous attitude or desire to see suffering and illness in the lives
of others. It was merely a result of my personal struggle to frame
the world in a realistic perspective, rather than the sugarcoated
delusions of a child. Certainly, 40 years of practicing medicine
provided an adequate background and the building blocks to
construct this imagery.

Despite the impressive achievements of modern medicine and
the seemingly miraculous cures of a few, we all know we are
headed down the same road. Even Gilgamesh, the god-like king

of Uruk around 2700 BC, was unable to obtain immortality by staying awake for six days as commanded by Utnapishtim. Ponce de Leon wasn't much help either with his failed search for the Fountain of Youth. Nevertheless, these historical failures have not stopped modern men from aspiring to avoid death indefinitely. In 1967, Robert Ettinger founded the cryonics (cryogenic hibernation) movement, which advocated the possibility of indefinitely preserving life by deep-freezing the body with liquid nitrogen. According to Larry Thompson of the National Genome Institute, there will be substantial hurdles to overcome with this technique. No one has ever successfully been unfrozen and brought back to life. But this hasn't deterred at least 100 souls, along with several dogs and cats, from their body being frozen and stored for possible future re-warming. This includes the body of one of the most famous athletes of all time, baseball legend Theodore Samuel (Ted) Williams. When he died in 2002, his family had his body transported to Scottsdale, Arizona, where it was frozen and stored.

The cryonics movement is too far-fetched for me to buy into. But I guess it may provide some real, albeit misguided, hope for the family. There is some scientific feasibility of recreating long extinct species from their salvaged DNA. But that's a totally different concept. In July of 2018, a group of Russian scientists successfully resuscitated two worms frozen in the Siberian tundra for 42,000 years in one case, and 32,000 years in another. They were both nematodes (round worms), panagrolaimus detritophagus and plectus parvus. If only worms could talk, we might hear the rest of the story. "Well, I just lay down for a nap and when I woke up, 42,000 years had passed. Where does the time go"? But this is silly. Worms are not people. And, in most cases, people are not worms. In any case, I was not obsessed with immortality. I was struggling to see humanity and individuals from a historical perspective. What comes to one must come to us all.

I believe I can best illustrate my frame of mind by citing an example. In mid-December 2019, I was driving to Harris Teeter to buy groceries when I tuned my radio to 104.7 FM. As a result, I heard Dean Martin crooning "A Marshmallow World" in his smooth and undeniably unique style. While this is far from being my favorite Christmas song, I found myself somewhat engrossed in the music. How does he produce those silky tones with so little effort? At the same time, this experience unleashed a whole new train of thought. Dean Martin, who was born Dino Paul Crocetti in Steubenville, Ohio, on June 7, 1917, and died Christmas Day 1995, is known as "The King of Cool" and as "Dino Martino." He is easily one of the most admired and successful entertainers of the mid-20th century. His greatest hits, including "Memories Are Made of This," "That's Amore," "Volare," and "Return to Me," are classics still enjoyed today. In 1964, "Everybody Loves Somebody Sometime" peaked at number one on the Billboard Hot 100 chart for a week, ousting the Beatles from that honor. If that's not enough notoriety, he also starred in a number movies and television shows with Jerry Lewis, plus a few box offices hits such as *Airport, Rio Bravo, Ocean's Eleven* and *The Cannonball Run.* You may admire Dino and regard him as Elvis Presley did: the coolest man who ever lived. Or you may think he projects an image of intoxication and irresponsibility. Either way, you can't deny the impressions he made, even a quarter-century after his death. My point is that he left his footprint in the universe. No one can erase it or change it. It is what it is. Now I am not suggesting that either the typical reader or I will leave a footprint in the universe as noteworthy as Dean Martin. But a footprint, for good or for ill, we shall leave. With a little luck, I'm hoping I can break even. As for Dino, I have to admit I kind of liked him, intoxicated or not.

With these philosophical thoughts flitting in and out of my conscious mind, I parked my car at Harris Teeter as "A Marshmallow World" concluded. I walked across the parking lot in a meditative state while trying to remember what five things I was supposed to buy. I could only think of four. Once in the store, I roamed the aisles to accomplish my mission. Finally, I remembered to get the bacon. But as I strolled to the meat department, I couldn't ignore the music blaring overhead: Dean Martin singing "A Marshmallow World." I'm not superstitious or a believer in ghosts, but maybe these metaphysical footprints are getting a little out of control.

This new way of looking at the world actually began well before retirement. But as full retirement became a daily reality, it seemed to become a stronger, more permanent fixture. Although it may have made me somewhat more detached, I can offer no apology. As René Descartes declared, "I think, therefore I am." I applied the same detached analysis to myself as I did to others, minimizing my personal biases as much as possible. Exactly how this worked is difficult to explain without being overly abstruse.

I will illustrate this phenomenon with some personal adventures from the summer of 2018 in the Greenbrier area. Rebecca and I noticed in July that the upstairs Goodman HVAC unit in our cabin was not cooling efficiently. I returned to the cabin mid-August for an appointment with the repairman. Apparently, coolant had been leaking from the condenser, so he replaced the condenser. That seemed to fix the problem. With my mission accomplished, I elected to eat out that evening at the Ship's Pub, an English-style pub only a few miles away. There I ordered a Killian's Irish Red Lager and shepherd's pie consisting of chicken and mushrooms in a white sauce. I believe it came with a side salad. Satisfied with my meal, I returned to the cabin about an hour later and went to bed around 9:00. I was in no big hurry to return home to Concord, but planned to head back mid-morning next day.

Unfortunately, I have developed in later life something resembling mild lactose intolerance. Sometimes after consuming food in a white sauce or other milk-based concoctions, I develop GI distress with diarrhea or loose stools. That evening, I got out of bed twice with this problem. But, by the next morning, I felt revived. My morning coffee cleared my mind and gave me new ambitions. I thought it would be nice to do a short run down by the Little Pigeon River before driving back to North Carolina. So, I donned my Nikes and gym shorts, anticipating a brief but vigorous workout. Just one more visit to the bathroom, then I was out the door.

There are many scenic roads for jogging in the Greenbrier area and, in fact, several high school cross country teams visit the park in late summer to train for the upcoming fall season. We have seen scores of teenagers running up or down Greenbrier Road in the park in various states of agony and ecstasy. Just a few years ago, I would run from my cabin up Greenbrier Road to the ranger station and back, a four-mile round trip through paradise. As I neared 70 years of age, however, this feat was a stretch. My new favorite place to run was on Emerts Cove Road, along the river where the terrain was relatively flat. I might do a slow jog around the loop, about 2.8 miles, or do a few shorter sprints on a flat straight portion of the road. There was a 300-yard flat section just north of the covered bridge that fit the need. Lined by rhododendrons, and with a view of Mt. Le Conte, one would be hard-pressed to find a more idyllic venue for the self-inflicted torture of a brief sprint workout. That morning, I decided to do three or four 250-yard runs, depending on how I felt.

A vigorous workout as a younger man in my 30s, 40s, or even 50s, was not an especially noteworthy endeavor. You "just do it," without any fear of injury or physical repercussions, or delusions of grandeur or self-righteousness. At almost 70, however, I tended to elevate the experience in my consciousness as a virtuous, historic, and almost spiritual event. You never know when it may be your last. Given my new way of viewing the world, I projected the following scenario:

Date: August 15, 2018

Time: 7:30 a.m.

Name: William Cottrell

Species: Homo sapiens

Height: 5' 11" (Okay, maybe 5' 10.5")

Weight: 79.0 kg (174 lbs.)

BMI: 24.6

Specialty: Middle distance runner

Past Honors: Member of Farragut High School's two-mile relay team that set school record in 1967. Took second place in 880-yard run intramural meet, University of Tennessee 1968, Knoxville, Tennessee. Several top three finishes in the Frost Bite 5K for my age group in my mid-60s, Kannapolis, North Carolina.

Career Goals: A top three finish in the 800-meter run for my age group in the Intergalactic Olympics to be held in the Alpha Centauri solar system, 2022.

Naturally, I would like to win the 800-meter race at Alpha Centauri, but I didn't want to appear over-confident or too egotistical about it. Third place would be okay. Today, I could possibly do a little more than my 250-yard sprints (225 m) with a slow jog in between, but I didn't want to peak too soon before the Olympics. I began my workout by slowly jogging down the 250-yard straight stretch, dangling my arms and looking around me to admire the scenery. It was a pleasant morning with the temperature in the low 70s, low humidity, and a partly cloudy blue sky framing the outline of Mt. Le Conte in the background.

I saw no evidence of paparazzi or other spectators; somehow, I had avoided their attention.

When I reached the end of the stretch, I did a slow 180-degree turn and headed back in the direction from which I came. As I did so, I began to slowly accelerate until in about 30 yards, I leveled off in a full sprint, probably about 90 percent of my possible maximum speed. I maintained this speed for the next 200 yards, slowing down a little as I neared the end. At this point, I stopped for a few seconds to re-evaluate the situation. As expected, I was a little winded. But I also experienced a little queasiness. Something was a tad off, and I wasn't quite sure what.

With these messages bombarding my control center, the term "recalculate" kept entering my consciousness. So, I made an executive decision. Doing four sprints was out. Just one more would be adequate; no need to press my luck. Feeling good about my ability to adapt to the situation, I slowly jogged back to the other end of the stretch to begin my second and final sprint. As I commenced my second sprint, I felt a bit light-headed, but otherwise not too bad. I challenged myself to keep up with an imaginary runner passing me on the right—maybe an alien from Alpha Centauri, trying to claim my medal.

Damn those aliens—if I could only—only—only—I opened my eyes slowly. The pavement felt warm on my face and I sensed a slight pain on my right knuckles and arm. What was I doing lying flat on the road? As I came to my senses, I realized I had blacked out. Why? I slowly rose to my hands and knees. I assumed a kneeling position for another minute or two, slowly raising my torso halfway and placing my hands on my knees before assuming a fully erect posture following another brief spell. I felt a warm burning sensation in my right cheek area and a mild pain over my right eyebrow. It really wasn't too bad. The worst pain came from the abrasions on my knuckles. Ouch!

As I became fully oriented, I analyzed the situation. I had a syncopal spell (blackout) while running near full speed. I didn't slip or lose my balance, nor was I pushed by anyone or chased by a bear or mad dog. It was all me. Also noteworthy was the fact that I have done similar workouts hundreds, if not thousands, of times without blacking out either partially or completely. What was different about today? I mentally reviewed my activities for the last 24 hours. The previous night, I had consumed a 12-ounce beer, but no water or other beverage. That morning, I had a cup of coffee, but no juice or other liquids. In addition, I had three episodes of loose stools, two in the middle of the night and one that morning. No brainer! I was dehydrated, at least mildly. At the same time, I was putting myself through a strenuous exercise test. In my mind I deduced the following axiom: 70 years of age + dehydration + strenuous exercise = syncope or some other dysfunction. Feeling confident that I had analyzed the situation appropriately, I slowly walked the half-mile back to my cabin. As I strolled along, I glanced at my watch: 7:45 a.m. I had been on Emerts Cove Road only about 15 minutes. Sometimes life can turn on a dime.

When I arrived at the cabin, my first action was to pour myself a tall glass of lemonade, then another, and finally a third. It was the best lemonade I have ever consumed either before or since. Dehydration is an underappreciated nemesis to humanity. People who are chronically dehydrated due to working in excessive heat, like the sugarcane workers of El Salvador, have a very high incidence of chronic kidney disease. Dehydrated patients undergoing anesthesia are more prone to have an unstable blood pressure than those adequately hydrated. Given the average adult body is about 60 percent water by weight, an 80 kg man would be about 48 kg (106 lbs.) of water. Therefore, a one-pound loss of body weight would constitute roughly one percent dehydration. Dysfunction progresses with the percentage of water loss. A one percent deficiency causes thirst. A five percent shortfall produces a fever. A 10 percent dearth will cause immobility. And a 12 to 15 percent loss will result in death. I estimate that I had a two or three percent water deficit at the time of my syncope. This is just a guess, however. I have known people to lose four or five pounds of water with vigorous activity, such as running or playing tennis, in hot, humid weather. That is serious business. Frequent rehydration with water, Gatorade or other fluids is extremely important.

My actions at this point were purely my own decision. I am merely describing what I did. In no way am I advocating people to follow my example. For most people, calling an ambulance or a doctor for consultation would be the most appropriate action. After rehydrating myself with lemonade, I viewed my face in the bathroom mirror. There was a two-centimeter gash over my right eye, and an ugly bruise already starting to form under and around the eye. Blood slowly dripped down my face. I had halfway considered telling my wife that I had tripped while running, and just cover the wound with an over-sized Band-Aid. Not only would that not have worked, but also it would be against all medical wisdom and advice. I had a full blackout. Even though I felt fine and was sure it was an exercise-induced event facilitated by my state of dehydration, I knew almost every medical center physician would be compelled to do a full-scale workup on my heart to rule out a conduction defect or blockages in my coronary arteries. If I drove to LeConte Medical Center in Sevierville, 30 minutes away, they would either admit me or send me by ambulance back to Concord, North Carolina, to Atrium Health Cabarrus, over 200 miles away. So, what should I do? Drive 30 minutes to Sevierville and enter the ER? Or call an ambulance to take me to Sevierville or all the way to Concord? Or maybe somebody could send a helicopter and pick me up on the roof of my house? My decision: I got in my car and drove four hours back to Concord. After I was well on my way, I called my wife to tell her what happened. I drove slowly and cautiously and was fully alert. The only problem I had driving back was another episode of GI distress requiring me to pull over in Shelby. Thank goodness for McDonald's.

When I arrived home, my wife drove me to the ER at Atrium Health Cabarrus, just over a mile from our house. From the ER I was admitted to the hospital for two days for a series of tests and an evaluation by the cardiologist. This is exactly what I expected would happen, so I made sure I had on clean underwear. I received top-notch care and was treated with the utmost respect. All my cardiac tests turned out okay. This was no big surprise. There was only one discovery that caught me off guard. The CT scan of my head showed four or five fractures in my right cheek area, one of which was just below the eye. Fortunately, none of the bones were displaced so I did not need surgery. I was also fortunate not to develop any infection or damage to the eye itself. All in all, it wasn't so bad. There was, however, a little drama when being evaluated in the ER. My rate heart was in the low 40s. That meant, with some expected variation due to respirations, it would briefly drop down into the 30s for a few seconds before returning back to the 40s. As this is well below average and I'd had a syncopal spell of uncertain cause, one physician mentioned that I might need a pacemaker. That was not an unreasonable consideration, given my circumstances, but it caught me by surprise. I had always believed that my cardiovascular system was among my greatest strengths. I have always possessed a heart rate well below average for as long as I can remember, which includes back in my college days. In young adults, a slow heart rate, say below 60 beats per minute, usually indicates an efficient cardiovascular system. The heart pumps more blood with each beat and therefore can pump a normal amount of blood each minute with a fewer number of contractions. While this may also be true with senior patients, i.e., 65 and older, it does become a little more complicated.

As people age, they are increasingly prone to develop problems with the nerve conduction system that signals the heart muscle to contract. So, a slow heart rate could be due to a defective conduction system, i.e., pathologic, or it could merely be due to more efficient contractions, i.e., physiologic. Distance runners and cyclists tend to have slow heart rates due to superb cardiovascular conditioning. Lance Armstrong allegedly has a baseline heart rate of approximately 35 beats per minute. Because I was quite active for my age, I strongly believed my slow heart rate was a good thing, that it was physiologic. The other problem I experienced was low back spasms of uncertain cause. I mentioned to someone that it reminded me of the sensation I had with a kidney stone. If dehydration can make one prone to syncope, it can also increase the possibility of developing a kidney stone. I did not, however, have the tenderness to palpation in my lower back that occurs classically with kidney stones. The back pains waxed and waned for no obvious reason. Tylenol helped somewhat but, for the most part, I was at the mercy of an unknown evil force.

After two days with little sleep, I was anxious to return home. The good news was that no serious problem was found with my heart. I was, however, scheduled to have a CT of the heart as an outpatient to rule out calcium deposits in my coronary arteries and a follow-up visit with the cardiologist in six months. All that checked out just fine too. There are no guarantees in life, but it seems unlikely that I am going to die of heart disease anytime soon. Yet my back spasms continued even after I returned home, though they weren't quite as severe. The next day, after a good night's sleep and more fluids, I needed to empty my bladder. Shortly after that I stood up and stretched and noticed the back pain rapidly dissipate. What a relief! It felt like the same relief I had several years ago when I passed a stone.

It has now been well over two years since this blackout spell occurred. I have been fine without further syncope or near syncopal events, despite vigorous exercise. I am, I admit, more careful about staying well hydrated. I confess that, despite this humbling series of events, I still continue to view myself—and my world—from a detached perspective. I see others and myself as transient beings, playing a role on a stage before bowing out. Although many are anxious to claim their 15 minutes of fame, they might be better off just wishing for a safe passage. Personally, I no longer fantasize about participating in the Alpha Centauri Olympics. But, if I feel up to it, I might consider competing in the Frost Bite 5K in nearby Kannapolis at some point.

2019, THE YEAR OF GRETA THUNBERG

But the line dividing good and evil cuts through the heart
of every human being. And who is willing to destroy a piece
of his own heart?

—*Aleksandr Solzhenitsyn*

The year 2018 had its share of misadventure; I could only hope 2019 would be a little more user-friendly. By January, my face had totally healed with only mild tenderness on the right side. The cabin's upstairs Goodman HVAC worked fine with the new condenser, but now we discovered a slow leak in the downstairs unit. I elected to merely add more coolant, while I tried to decide whether to replace the condenser or at some time replace one or both units entirely. Hard to believe the cabin would soon be 14 years old. The major 2019 news events centered around the Mueller report, concerning Russia's probable involvement in the 2016 election, and the presidential impeachment proceedings initiated by the House of Representatives because of Trump's suspected illegal dealings with the Ukraine. Controversy about illegal immigration, the U.S.-Mexico border wall, and school shootings continued. In late 2019, the raging bush fires in Australia gained increased media coverage. Ever in the background were a growing number of reports related to climate change. I frequently amused myself by reading about the most recent form of devastation attributed to a warming planet.

There seemed to be a cycle of several articles portraying gloom and doom in the coming decades, interspersed with an occasional article minimizing these concerns. As the year progressed, however, the latter became less frequent. According to a poll conducted by the Kaiser Family Foundation and reported in *The Washington Post* on September 13, 2019, roughly eight out of ten people believe human activity is contributing to climate change. And then there was Greta Thunberg, *Time* magazine's "Person of the Year" for 2019. According to *Time*, Thunberg has become "The biggest voice on the biggest issue facing the planet." In elementary school, she watched a video about extreme weather, flooding, and starving polar bears, and she became alarmed. At age 11, she became severely depressed. Her family consoled her and changed their lifestyle to decrease their CO_2 emissions. Eventually, she recovered and became avidly proactive on the political scene. In May 2018, at age 15, Thunberg wrote an essay about climate change that was published in a Swedish newspaper and garnered national attention. Then emulating the high school students in Parkland, Florida, who protested gun violence with organized school strikes, Thunberg organized a school strike in front of the Swedish Parliament. On the first day, August 20, 2018, she was alone. Eventually, hundreds, then thousands, of fellow protesters joined her in her strike.

This Skolstrejk for Klimatet—school strike for climate change—started by just one young person in Sweden in August 2018, spawned a series of school strikes globally throughout 2019. Thunberg gained international attention and was invited to speak to the heads of state at the United Nations General Assembly. She was also a guest speaker at the World Economic Forum in Davos, Switzerland. Despite wide acclaim, she has been mocked and criticized by heads of state including Jair Bolsonaro of Brazil, and Donald Trump. Thunberg needs police protection when traveling due to threats to her and her family. But what do the obsessions of a 17-year-old girl, a barely five-foot-tall child with Asperger syndrome, have to do with my life in the Greenbrier? Maybe very little in the immediate time frame. Then again, maybe everything in the future. Either way, it seems our country's youth have highjacked the important global issues of our time with their protests. How dare they! They also claim the right to go to school without fear of being shot, and that they also are fighting for their right to inherit a livable planet for themselves and their children. Maybe they are all spoiled brats? I have attempted to objectively analyze the arguments and evidence that support the case for climate change, especially global warming, and look for weaknesses and contradictions. There are quite a few.

In 2000, a possibly flawed study based on measuring tree rings of the huon pine tree in Tasmania distorted evidence for the Little Ice Age and the Modern Warming. Also in 2000, the infamous "Hockey Stick "graph of the average temperature in the Northern Hemisphere for the last millennium was published by American climatologist and geophysicist Michael Mann. By combining data from several different sources, the chart appears to exaggerate temperature rise in the 20th century, making the sudden rise resemble the end of a hockey stick. Though commonly acknowledged as flawed by many, these atypical reports are still used as ammunition by climate change deniers. Other people point to alarmists who exaggerate the immediate threat of warming by predicting the end of life on earth as we know it to occur in just a few years. Likewise, some people weaponize specific events like fires or hurricanes by claiming they are primarily a result of global warming. This tends to undermine their credibility. As true scientists realize, global warming is not a perpetrator; rather, it is a conspirator. A warmer environment merely helps make some events slightly more probable. Furthermore, as still others will point out, a mere consensus of leading scientists does not constitute proof.

Analyzing the causes of climate change is truly a multivariate nightmare. However logical and probable, the theory that global warming is due to anthropogenic (man-made) greenhouse gases lacks irrefutable proof on the most basic level. Analyzing and critiquing the claims of climate deniers, however, is even more productive. Bound only by their skepticism of modern climate scientists, they lack a cohesive, credible counterargument. Some claim variation in solar activity is responsible for climate change, despite denial of this by NASA and others. Others claim that increasing levels of CO_2 and a warmer environment will be good for humanity. Still others deny that a warming trend even exists. While all these deficiencies weaken their claims, they are a diminishing but resilient lot. I can't totally dismiss these irascible diehards, but I do believe their heyday has passed. I search for validation from historic analogies.

The link between smoking and lung cancer is well established today. Despite the fact that medical research had documented concern about tobacco in the 1950s, consumers did not benefit from this news in a timely manner. This is largely because the tobacco industry sponsored a disinformation campaign by paying a select group of scientists to raise objections to the validity of the scientific link. In some cases, they were the same scientists who cast doubt on the importance of acid rain and global warming. At times, the government appeared to be complicit. These behind-the-scenes connections, of course, don't prove anything, per se, but they certainly raise a red flag.

The story of lead toxicity in the 20th century is equally disconcerting. In 1921, it was discovered that adding lead in the form of tetraethyl lead would decrease shuddering, also known as engine knock, when added to gasoline. So, in 1923, General Motors, Du Pont, and Standard Oil formed a joint enterprise called Ethyl Corporation to market as much tetraethyl lead (aka, ethyl) worldwide as they were able. Despite early cases of neurotoxicity, five deaths, and 35 cases of severe toxicity from one facility in 1924, the company continued to deny any problems with their product. Lead was also used to seal food cans and for water storage tanks. Despite rumors of problems, the company's leaders denied a problem. As late as 2001, Ethyl executives continued to contend that research had failed to show a threat to either humans or the environment from their product.

Enter American geochemist Clair Patterson who, in 1953, was the first scientist to accurately estimate the age of the earth at about 4.55 billion years. Perhaps the most influential scientist you haven't heard of, Patterson, who was on faculty at California Institute of Technology (Caltech) for four decades, made his estimate from studying the ratio of lead to uranium in ancient rocks and meteorites. While measuring lead levels, however, he soon learned that his rock samples were contaminated with lead from the atmosphere. In other words, he discovered that earth's atmosphere unexpectedly contained a lot of lead. He was able to show that these levels increased dramatically after 1923, when lead was added to gasoline, by analyzing the content of lead in layers of ice in Greenland. Armed with this knowledge, Patterson began a tedious campaign to have lead removed from gasoline. As a result, both the American Petroleum Institute and the United States Public Health Service canceled his research contracts. The Ethyl Corporation itself refused to endow a chair at Caltech unless Patterson was removed first. Ultimately, Patterson was successful in the Clean Air Act being passed in 1970 and in removing leaded gasoline from the U.S. in 1986. Lead levels in Americans dropped dramatically soon thereafter. Surprisingly, modest amounts of ethyl were still marketed overseas, even after the year 2000. Unfortunately, Clair Patterson, who died in December 1995, never gained any special recognition for his achievements.

Perhaps it should not be too surprising that science and industry are so often at odds. As Canadian author, social activist, and filmmaker Naomi Klein commented in her 2014 book, *This Changes Everything: Capitalism vs. The Climate*, 2014, "The bottom line is that we are all inclined to denial when the truth is too costly—whether emotionally, intellectually or financially." American writer Upton Sinclair (1878 – 1968) similarly observed: "It is difficult to get a man to understand something when his salary depends on his not understanding it." Perhaps these disputes are less of an aberration and more a hallmark of history. Speaking truth to power has always been a recurrent challenge for society.

Rebecca and I decided to finish out the year with a brief visit to Greenbrier. She left for the cabin on the 28th of December, and I drove up on New Year's Eve. No big celebration was necessary, just a gin and tonic and a home-cooked meal would do. With the year coming to a close, however, we reminded ourselves of one minor adventure in the area we considered but never accomplished: visiting the actual birthplace and childhood home of Dolly Parton on Locust Ridge—the inspiration for her famous song, "My Tennessee Mountain Home," and a concept album released in 1973. We had seen the Parton cabin's replica in Dollywood, but now we wanted to see the real thing.

Mid-morning on New Year's Day 2020, we left our cabin and headed north on State Road 416, which more or less follows the Little Pigeon River as it winds its way north toward the French Broad River. Our GPS indicated the home was just over 11 miles from our cabin. I estimated it was probably six or seven miles as the crow flies. Not only were the roads curvier than Dolly herself, but the route also took us a mile or so past Locust Ridge to the bridge at Richardson Cove, and then a series of narrow roads took us to Evans Chapel Road. When the GPS indicated we were less than 0.2 miles from our destination, we pulled over and parked next to some mountain condos.

We got out and looked around. No signs or arrows pointed the way. I saw a footpath leading up a steep hill, so we hiked up a few hundred yards. All we saw were a bunch of old abandoned Ford 9000 dump trucks and an incomplete foundation of somebody's abandoned vacation home, and the GPS now indicated 0.3 miles. So, we regrouped. Eventually we headed down an unmarked inconspicuous road for about a quarter-mile. At the bottom there was a beautiful babbling brook and verdant hillside, but no little mountain home. Then I noticed, off to my left, a 12-foot-high wooden privacy fence. It extended on both sides well up the hill. I peeked through the slats and saw a beautifully manicured field and well cared for grounds and outbuildings. No brainer—this was Dolly Parton's childhood homestead! Only the house itself was difficult to see. We considered trying to scale the fence or hike around it, but opted against both. Maybe there were hidden cameras, or worse.

I couldn't help but wonder what Dr. Robert Thomas was thinking on January 19, 1946, when he was called to deliver a baby at the Parton home. Just where did he and his horse cross the river to get to Locust Ridge? And could he have ever imagined the baby he delivered that day would become one of the most famous country entertainers of all time? We wandered around the fence for about 30 minutes, trying to imagine what it was like to grow up in this rural setting. I was reminded of what Dolly said about her childhood home: "We always had running water. Whenever we needed water, we would run and get it." Perhaps not everyone may appreciate her down-home humor. But I really don't think she would mind that we were trying to get a better look at her Tennessee Mountain Home. and say "Hello, Dolly."

THE SECRETS OF WATER

When the well's dry, we learn the worth of water.

—Benjamin Franklin

Visiting Dolly Parton's childhood homestead reminded me of the water challenges rural communities faced, even in my lifetime, and how various practices evolved. Using spring water and outhouses may have seemed to work okay for many, but when Dr. Thomas arrived in Greenbrier in 1926, he was shocked to find many cases of typhoid, diphtheria, scarlet fever, tuberculosis, and even a few cases of smallpox. Medical treatment fell to granny women and their home remedies. Typhoid fever, in particular, is a potentially deadly disease spread by contaminated water. A person can contract the disease by ingesting as little as 1,000 bacteria. Just as John Snow argued in 1849 during the cholera epidemic in London, contamination of drinking water with sewage is frequently the underlying problem. All this was well known by medical science when Dr. Thomas arrived, but primitive superstitious practices were still common.

Medical epidemiologists and doctors learned a great deal about the spread of typhoid in the late 19th century from two cities in Massachusetts, Lowell and Lawrence, both located on the Merrimack River and developed in the mid-1800s as mill towns powered by waterwheels. The larger city of Lowell, population

78,000, was about ten miles upstream from Lawrence, population 45,000. In 1890, a major typhoid epidemic hit both cities infecting about 1,500 people and causing 233 deaths that year. Investigators traced the source to Stony Brook, a small stream entering the Merrimack a few miles further upstream. Lowell was able to solve their problem by using groundwater instead of the river for their water source. Unfortunately, Lawrence lacked an adequate groundwater source.

At the time, most authorities believed in the concept of self-purification. As water flowed downstream, the combined effects of sunlight and oxidation as the water mixed with air would eventually make it safe to drink. It was permissible for sewage to be dumped directly into rivers as long as the intakes for domestic use weren't too close. Unfortunately for Lawrence, their distance from the source was inadequate to do the job of self-purification. Eventually, with the help of engineers from nearby MIT and the Massachusetts State Department of Health, an effective sand filtration process was developed that removed the culprit, salmonella typhi bacteria, as well as a number of other pathogens. The filters were so effective that Allen Hazen (1869 – 1930), a graduate of Dartmouth College at age 15, concluded, "For every death from typhoid fever avoided by the purification of public water supplies, two or three deaths are avoided from other causes." This is known as Hazen's theorem.

The example of stopping typhoid fever serves as sort of a proxy for solving water problems in general. Each city has its own unique dilemmas and solutions to involve the treatment of sewage and of clean water sources. And, of course, contaminants include copious infective agents, as well as lead, organic wastes, industrial waste, pesticides, medical products, and potential carcinogens. As recently as 1900, both Philadelphia and Washington, D.C. dumped sewage above the intake. Such practices are unheard of today. Trillions of dollars have been spent worldwide to make water safer for human consumption.

There seems to be a trend, whenever possible, to resort back to local water sources and disposal systems as opposed to always accessing a centralized water or sewage network. Also, as usual, concern over trace chemicals as potential carcinogens is seemingly never-ending. The art and science of water management is always adapting to the new challenge. However, I just recently learned the Trump Administration is rolling back controls on water pollution. Maybe that's good if you own 15 golf courses, but I'm not sure about the rest of us. Many people in this country can go a lifetime without a water failure or contamination problem. And that is a luxury we too often take for granted. How long will it last?

Dr. Richard Wolfenden is a biochemistry professor at the University of North Carolina at Chapel Hill and a noted water expert. Charles Fishman, author of *The Big Thirst,* asked him about our future relationship with water. After a brief silence, Wolfenden replied: "I think our relationship with water is going to be one of the deciding things of the next century. I don't think water's in any trouble. But we might be." Many people refer to our water problem as a global water crisis or a global water shortage, just as they might refer to a global climate crisis or a global economic crisis. While this is understandable, it is somewhat misleading. Most all water problems are local and require individualized solutions. Converting seawater to fresh water with a desalination plant may be a viable solution in Perth, Australia, and Carlsbad, California, recycling and water restrictions is perfect for Las Vegas, Nevada, and engineering projects to bring water from the nearby Catskill Mountains (aka, the Catskills) is an efficient solution for New York City. However, there is no one-size-fits-all solution. Furthermore, rarely can a surplus of water in one location readily alleviate a shortage in another.

In 2008, Barcelona, Spain, faced a crisis when an 18-month-long drought left their reservoirs almost empty. Barcelona paid millions in Euros for tankers to ship loads of water from Tarragona, Spain, and Marseille, France. Not only were these supplies short-lived (one tankful lasted less than an hour), but they were also a financial burden. Fortunately, major rains soon solved the dilemma. Most people don't realize that the earth's total water supply is constant. All the earth's water is thought to have formed about 4.5 billion years ago, shortly after the earth itself was formed. All of our planet's water was created in outer space from cosmic molecules of hydrogen, the most common element, and oxygen. None has been created or lost since. But, of course, it has changed forms and locations continuously. All H_2O molecules have cycled through the foulest, most disgusting spots as well as the cleanest. Not necessarily a pleasant thought.

Everyone is aware that water is important for life, but most lack an appreciation of the full extent. For example, the presence of H_2O in a living cell determines the shape and activities of protein molecules, which, in turn, manage most of a body's functions. The unique polarity of the water molecule, with a slight positive charge on the hydrogen atom and a slight negative charge on the oxygen, results in many properties including its role as a universal solvent. Furthermore, water's unique property of expanding when cooled to solid form, and not contracting like most other substances, is key to the existence of life as we know it. Since ice forms on the surface of lakes and other bodies of water, instead of the bottom (which would happen if ice were denser), it prevents the whole lake from freezing, and therefore gives aquatic life a much better chance for survival in winter. Most people likely realize that water is the only substance that exists in three states (solid, liquid, and gas) on earth, but few people appreciate how its mass is distributed. Our planet's total surface water, including oceans, lakes, glaciers, and atmospheric H_2O, accounts for only 0.025 percent of its total mass. Most of the rest is locked up in the earth's mantle, about 250,000 – 400,000 miles below the earth's surface. This H_2O is chemically dispersed under high pressure throughout the rock's structure. It doesn't resemble normal water in this condition, but when the pressure is reduced, the water will exit the hydrated minerals. This is what happens when a volcano erupts and spews lava. Its mineral-locked water is believed to help stabilize the ocean's water level and also facilitate continental drift or plate tectonics. Who'd have thought that most of the earth's water would exist so far below the earth's surface in the form of hydrated minerals or watery rocks?

Many of Man's water challenges were exacerbated when he transitioned to an agrarian lifestyle roughly 11,000 to 12,000 years ago. Before that time, tribes would roam the earth to find the best game and vegetation for consumption (i.e., Man was a hunter-gatherer). Long-term sewage disposal was less of a problem because of the transient nature of the tribes' settlements. Most people would assume that becoming more established in farming communities would lead to a more desirable lifestyle, but this was not always the case. Israeli historian, Yuval Noah Harari, in his 2014 science bestseller, *Sapiens: A Brief History of Humankind,* makes the bold argument that claiming the agrarian revolution improved the quality of life is history's biggest fraud. Families had more children, but infant mortality was very high. There was less uncertainty about where one would live, but occasional crop failures and diseases were unavoidable. Harari even asserts that Man didn't domesticate wheat, but rather wheat domesticated Man, who had to jump through hoops for the benefit of the plant. Furthermore, the lack of a more varied diet was not beneficial.

The Cherokee Indians who lived in East Tennessee and Western North Carolina were both farmers and hunter-gatherers. They raised corn, beans, and squash, and supplemented with wild greens, nuts, berries, and wild game and fish. They occasionally may have dug latrines, but had no sophisticated sewage disposal system. Even so, it is probable sanitation problems were not as bad for the Cherokee as in European cities in the 1700s and 1800s.

I grew up in a time and culture in which sanitary practices, such as city sewer systems and septic tanks, were the norm for sewage disposal and water use. I can recall an occasional an "ole timey" outhouse, but they were the exception. Even though my father was a water commissioner for our utility district, I took these advantages for granted. Only during medical school and later did I begin to appreciate the enormous health implications of safe water and sewage systems. The life span of the average American increased from age 47 to 63 between 1900 and 1947. About half of that increase was believed to be due to improvements in drinking water according to David Sedlak in his 2015 book, *Water 4.0: The Past, Present, and Future of the World's Most Vital Resource.*

A recent challenge for society has been the disposal of pet feces. This didn't seem to be a problem in my childhood in a rural setting. But the increased population density and leash laws in cities and suburbs make this issue critical. Indoor cats are usually not a big problem. Just provide a litter box and routinely purchase an adequate kitty litter, and even the most persnickety and arrogant feline will do their business in a clean and professional manner—at least, until they become old and senile like Belle, our last cat. Dogs are a little more of a challenge. I remember the first time I had to carry gloves and poop bags with me when we took our dogs to the park. I agreed with the need but found it more difficult to enjoy the outing. My main focus now is in removing the doggie poop from the yard, since we have two dogs and a limited backyard area, both at our Greenbrier cabin and our Concord home.

In addition to regular poop bags, there are now biodegradable ones (such as BioBag) and flushables (such as FlushEze). There are special devices that can connect an outside port directly to your sewer system (like Powerloo, an outdoor "dog toilet"), or waste digesters (like the Doggie Dooley, an in-ground disposal system for dog waste); adding water and enzymes helps liquefy the waste and return it to the earth, kind of a doggie septic tank. Or you could go all out and hire a pet waste removal service to make periodic visits. One local service is Charlotte Poop 911. Their phone number is 1-877-POOP-911 in case you need to get in touch. These services aren't my personal choice, but I'm guessing they do a great job.

Dog feces may not be as toxic as human feces, but nobody wants to step in it, so everybody needs to have some kind of system in place. Mine is not too complex or sophisticated. It requires the following equipment: 1) one glove, 2) one garden trowel, and 3) one strong arm. Simply load the trowel with dog poop using one gloved hand. Common sense dictates that it's better not to overdo it; half full is about right. The main risk is in overloading the trowel, which may result in an undesirable dispersion pattern. Then sling the poop using a rapid swinging motion, sort of like an underhanded softball pitch, but faster, over the fence or yard demarcation. Sidearm and backhand techniques are good alternatives for the more advanced slinger. Understandably, this system will not work if your yard does not abut on an adequate natural space without man-made structures. Do not discard onto your neighbor's property! Fortunately, both of our residences are in wooded areas. Unless you have a spastic arm, this technique should serve you well. The only other technical problem I have witnessed is when the doggie poop inadvertently crashes into a low-lying tree limb at the yard's edge. An occasional turd may roll back down the hill and re-enter the yard, requiring a second launch. Good technique and due diligence, however, can minimize this problem.

WILD SWIMMING

*Until we can understand the assumptions in which we are
drenched we cannot know ourselves.*

—Adrienne Rich

January 2020 marked not only the start of a new decade, but also the second anniversary of my full retirement as an anesthesiologist. If my life was a mile run, I was entering the last of four laps. No biggie, but a reason to take stock. A brief hike up Greenbrier Road is helpful to put things in perspective. Watching the turbulent water flowing over the rocks is mesmerizing; always different, but always the same. The simplest things are also the most extraordinary.

I am reminded that, in the year 2000, the Middle Prong of the Little Pigeon River was designated an "Outstanding Natural Resource Waterway" by the Tennessee Division of Pollution Control. Glen Cardwell, a native and author of *The Greenbrier Cove Story,* claims the stream earns a Blue Ribbon for its high standard of purity. He is quick to point out, however, that since wild hogs and other game use the stream for urinating and defecating, the park service does not recommend drinking the water untreated. That's because a single-celled parasite, giardiasis lamblia, and a spiral-shaped bacteria, leptospirosis, may cause serious gastrointestinal infections. I am sure I have swallowed gallons of this water over my lifetime without noticeable problems. Nevertheless, no one can say the water is safe to drink; so, it is wise to bring your own drinking water when hiking in the area. There are more than 300 streams in the park, of which 735 miles are classified as fishable. Average annual rainfall in the park is around 82 inches a year in the higher elevations. It is estimated that about 890 billion gallons of precipitation (rain, snow, sleet, fog, mist, and dew) fall on the park annually, and about 500 billion gallons of water flow out annually in streams. The average amount of water flowing out of the park in the Middle Prong, under the bridge on U.S. 321, is about two million gallons a day or 730 million gallons per year. The river is a scenic treasure and tame by most standards, but it wasn't always so.

In 1891, the Scottish Lumber Company cut down scores of mature trees: yellow poplar, basswood, maples, and others positioned on the banks of Porter Creek. A sudden cloudburst, however, swept the logs off the bank and scattered them along the riverbanks for miles downstream. The Emerts Cove School was totally destroyed. It was such a landmark natural disaster that, for years after, old-timers referred to events as happening before or after the flood. In 1938, there was another major flash-flood of the Little Pigeon River. This one resulted in the deaths of six people from the same family. I have never seen flooding even remotely as severe as these two deluges. The worst I witnessed was a rapid rise of three or four feet in a couple hours in the early 1970s. Most likely that was due to farming or logging having no longer been allowed in Greenbrier Cove since at least 1934. Beginning in 1955, when I first learned to swim in a relatively calm section of the river, I have revered the Middle Prong as a superb facility for innertubing and taking a refreshing dip. This aquatic activity, however, does have one minor drawback: the water is cold! Whereas in August the water temperature may rise to the low 70s, it is otherwise much colder. Everyone has a preferred technique for acclimation. Most people wade in very slowly, hugging themselves for warmth; others get a running start

and do a sudden headfirst emersion. Although I generally preferred the second method as a younger man, I am more cautious
today. If the water is extremely cold (60 degrees Fahrenheit or
below), hypothermia symptoms can occur.

The first stage of hypothermia results in hyperventilation
with blood pressure changes. Panic and drowning have been
reported. After a few minutes, superficial blood vessels in the
skin and muscles constrict, diverting more blood to the heart and
brain. When this happens, muscle activity in the arms and legs
can become sluggish. If submersion persists, decreased body temperature can lead to confusion and, ultimately, unconsciousness.
Understandably, drowning is possible at any stage, but more so
with weak swimmers. A pre-existing heart condition, like arryth-
mias or coronary blockages, makes hypothermia even more
dangerous. Because I grew up swimming in mountain waters,
I have become somewhat acclimated to swimming in cold temperatures. I have never done an ocean swim on New Year's Day,
like members of the Coney Island Polar Bear Club, but I stand
in awe of such audacity. I am usually among the last to swim
outdoors in the SportsCenter pool before it closes in late October.
Somehow the challenge suits me.

So, I was very interested in a recent article by Rebecca Mead
titled, "Going for the Cold," in *The New Yorker* magazine.
According to Mead, Britons have rediscovered the thrill of
swimming in cold lakes, rivers, and seas, a sport known officially
as "wild swimming." In 1973, a British writer, Roger Deakin,
restored Walnut Tree Farm, a rundown farmhouse in Suffolk
built in the 1500s. In addition to restoring the house, he had
the moat dredged and cleaned, and began using it routinely
for nature swims. He then proceeded to make a trek through
England, Wales, and Scotland, swimming in numerous bodies of
water for pleasure. His 1999 story of this adventure, *Waterlog:
A Swimmer's Journey Through Britain,* became widely acclaimed
as a nature classic. "Wild swimming" has grown rapidly in

popularity since the book's release. Sport England estimates about 500,000 people participate in wild swimming in Britain. Numerous local societies are dedicated to the sport. Most swims are done in groups at designated times and places. Bathing suits are optional, though some use wet suits for the extremely cold waters. The health benefits of wild swimming are controversial.

Advocates claim it has a mood elevating effect and gives them clarity of mind. Some individuals claim that it boosts their immune system, while others feel it may in some cases decrease inflammation. Dr. Mark Harper, of Brighton and Sussex University Hospitals, believes it may help some people handle daily stress better. That is, by learning to adapt to the stress of cold water, one may be better able to handle other stresses. Dr. Harper is a wild swimmer himself. The jury may still be out, but most swimmers are convinced that it creates a sense of well-being. If you need tips on safety or etiquette for wild swimming, check out the website of Outdoor Swimming Society, founded in 2006 by Kate Rew. Or take a look at her guidebook, *Wild Swim,* first released in 2008. Rich illustrations demonstrate the beauty and eccentricity of the sport and offer a number of suggestions for bodies of water to gain the experience. A review of history suggests wild swimming is nothing new, even if known by other names.

Allegedly, Julius Caesar was an excellent swimmer, and military training included the useful art of swimming both in the first century and Middle Ages. *De Arte Natandi,* written in 1587 by the English scholar Everad Digby, offers a historical perspective on the art of swimming or otherwise how to get around safely in water. It was also the British who eventually promoted competitive swimming and standardized modern swimming strokes.

Industrial pollution of waterways throughout the world became a major problem in the late-19th and early-20th centuries. As late as 1980, most of the UK's inland water did not meet the standards of the European Economic Community's Bathing

Water Directive. Much improvement has been made in the last 40 years. A similar pattern existed in our own country.

The Strait of Dardanelles is a narrow strip of water 38 miles long, and three-quarters of a mile to four miles wide. It has historically been known as the Hellespont and connects the Aegean and Mediterranean Sea with the Sea of Marmara and the Black Sea. Thus, it separates Europe (Ancient Greece) on the northwest side, and Asia (modern Turkey) on the southeast side. According to Greek mythology, Helle fell into the sea while fleeing her homeland when she lost her grip on the golden ram, hence the name "Hellespont" or the Sea of Helle. In later times, Leander, a mortal from the southeast side, swam the Hellespont nightly to meet his lover, Hero, a priestess of Aphrodite. Unfortunately, Leander lost his way one stormy night and drowned. It's no wonder that George Gordon Byron (Lord Byron to most) chose this body of water to accomplish one of the most famous wild swims of all times. While touring the Mediterranean in 1810, Byron swam the Hellespont, about four miles. He boasts of this swim in his poem, "Don Juan," and later claims it as his most noteworthy achievement. Although he had a highly unstable and tempestuous life, he is recognized as one of the icons of the Romantic Movement. In 1823, he left Italy for Greece, where he helped train Greek soldiers in their fight for independence from Turkey. Although he caught fever and died in 1824, he became a hero to the Greeks and a noted figure in English literature.

Most of my wild swims have been in mountain streams of the Appalachian Mountains. Whether swimming the Middle Prong or the Straits of Dardanelles, water safety is imperative. Extreme cold will greatly limit performance, so know your own limits. Possible pollution and wildlife are complicating factors. There is, however, a paradoxical reflex that can be relevant. The diving reflex, or diving response, is present to some degree in all mammals, but is especially pronounced in aquatic animals like seals and otters. When exposed to cold water, they automatically have a slowed heart rate and stop breathing; blood and oxygen is preferentially shunted to vital organs. This allows for a much longer submersion time by conserving oxygen stores. Although adult humans can display this reflex, it is much more pronounced in babies and infants. This helps explain why occasionally an infant submerged for 30 minutes or more has been resuscitated successfully. Paradoxically, hypothermia resulting from unusually cold water can slow metabolism and decrease anoxic damage (i.e., consequences of oxygen deprivation). Infants have a greater surface area to body mass ratio, which enhances cooling. Further, their brain cells and other tissues are more resilient than in adults. Nevertheless, these miracle resuscitations from cold-water drownings are the exception to the rule. Cold water can be extremely dangerous.

As I entered my third year of retirement, I was beginning to realize that my own pot of gold would most likely consist of my rich collection of personal encounters and experiences as opposed to any quixotic accomplishment or discovery. As noted in Coelho's *The Alchemist*, "The simple things in life are also the most extraordinary things, and only the wise can see them." How could I have known that, in the next few months, I would face some controversies that would make my past adventures seem like child's play?

DENDROCHRONOLOGY

Doubt is not a pleasant condition, but certainty is absurd.

—Francois Voltaire

The cove hardwood forest is but one of 11 distinct habitats in the Great Smokies, and is perhaps the most distinguishing feature of the Greenbrier area and much of the park. During growing-season, an old growth tree can transpire up to 900 gallons of water a day. When combined with aerosol particles of dust, smoke, salt crystals, and various hydrocarbons, this moisture can create the characteristic mountain haze. The Cherokee called it Shaconage, or "Land of the Blue Smoke." There were 18 lumber companies that harvested trees in the late-19th and early-20th centuries. The largest in acreage was the Champion Fiber Company, but their activities remained confined to the North Carolina side of the park. The only lumber company to work in the Greenbrier Cove area was the Scottish Lumber Company. After the big flood of 1891, however, they were forced to declare bankruptcy. Some of the biggest trees in the park are the tulip poplars in the cove hardwood of Greenbrier Cove. One measures nearly 40 feet in circumference and is 90 feet tall. However, the tallest poplar exceeds 190 feet in height and has a 24-foot circumference. A number of poplars here are around 500 years old. The forest immediately around Greenbrier Road is a succession forest, around 90 years old. It will take at least another 100 years to reach maturity since the original forest was cleared for farmland, and various settlements in Greenbrier, Injun Creek, Laurel Creek, Indian Nation, Horseshoe, Middle Prong, Cow Flats, West Prong, and Partontown clustered around rivers and creeks in this area.

Numerous trails emanate from Greenbrier Road to the old growth forest. Besides the Injun Creek Trail and the Laurel Creek Trail mentioned earlier, there is Porters Trail, especially appealing to wildflower lovers, and Ramsey's Cascade Trail, which leads to the highest waterfall in the park at 100 feet. This is also one of the best trails for seeing the old growth forest. Ramsey's Cascade Trail is slightly more than an eight-mile round trip and considered moderately strenuous. The trail gains almost 2,200 feet in elevation in four miles, ending at an elevation of 4,256 feet. No special skills or equipment are needed, but you can expect a fair amount of joint and muscle soreness unless you are a seasoned hiker. It is also noteworthy that climbing the falls is not recommended; several deaths have been reported.

The oldest tree in the Smokies is a blackgum tree at 562 years old. That means it started growing in 1438, two years before Johannes Gutenberg started perfecting the first printing press in Strasbourg, France, and 54 years before Columbus sailed the ocean blue. It's humbling to contemplate other life forms whose lifespan supersedes ours so profoundly. Unfortunately, I have been unable to discover the location of this distinguished tree.

These trees in the Smokies are neither the oldest nor the largest in the world by a longshot. Around 1900, the giant sequoias in California were thought to be the oldest at 3,000 years old. The General Sherman tree in Sequoia National Park is 25 feet in diameter and 275 feet tall. Although some redwoods in Northern California are taller, up to 370 feet, the famous giant sequoia is by far the biggest by volume.

Andrew Ellicott Douglass, an astronomer, seriously began to study tree rings in 1904 to look for a correlation between solar activity and tree ring width. He is credited with founding the science of dendrochronology—the dating of trees by number of rings. He also noted the width of the rings was prone to vary considerably with the type of weather for a particular year. A warm wet year produces a wider ring than in a cold dry year. In the 1940s, a forest ranger suggested the bristlecone pine in Eastern California might actually be older than the sequoias. This was verified in 1953 when Edmund Schulman extracted a narrow cylindrical sample of the tree with a boring device. By this method he determined some of the bristlecones were at least 4,500 years old. Later, one was found to be close to 5,000 years old. Dendrochronology is an undeniably fascinating science and, because of the correlation between climatic events and tree rings, the dates of some ancient events between 1700 and 1500 BC have been adjusted.

Understandably, dendrochronology has stirred up several controversies. In 1949, an American physical chemist at the University of Chicago named Willard Libby discovered the technique of determining the age of ancient materials by measuring how much radioactive isotope Carbon-14 they contained. Carbon-14 (or radiocarbon) has a half-life for disappearing at about 5,600 years; that means only 50 percent will be present after one half-life, 25 percent after two half-lives, and so on. This technique, known as radiocarbon dating or Carbon-14 dating, was so revered that Libby won the Nobel Prize in Chemistry in 1960. Despite its usefulness, however, the Carbon-14 dating method had potential flaws. If the sample was contaminated with nearby material, the reading could be made erroneous. The other weakness is that estimates depended on a consistent level of Carbon-14 in the atmosphere for accurate calculations. If past levels were much higher or lower, the age estimate would be thrown off.

In 1998, Michael Evan Mann, a well-respected climatologist, used tree ring data from bristlecone pines in the White Mountains of California to reconstruct past temperatures from about 1850. The resulting temperature graph reveals a sharp increase in the 20th century, somewhat like the end of a hockey stick. Mann later modified the study by consistently using trees from a higher elevation to get a more accurate reflection of climate variations. Others helped Mann refine his model of reconstruction and enabled him to confirm the upswing of temperatures, but climate change deniers claimed fraud. The struggle for credibility continues. These cases don't prove a failure of science, but rather are examples of how science is supposed to work. Theories about how the physical world works are proposed and examined. Frequently they are applauded for a period until a discrepancy is discovered, then the theory is refined or modified to compensate for the flaw. This is how understanding is advanced.

The ongoing debate between climatologists and climate change deniers, however, remains intense. About the time it seems scientific research has closed the deal for climatologists, some noteworthy politician, economist, or think tank will vociferously raise objections. Considering what's at stake, it is the critical issue of our times. This is disconcerting. All conflicts beg for resolution. As noted earlier, since retirement I have developed a tendency to objectify my life and interactions with other people. For better or worse, I view my daily activities from a detached perspective. The goal is to remove my personal biases and nuances from the picture in order to see things as they really are. But how could I do this with the climate change controversy? Everyone involved seems overly eager to push their own agenda. Science itself is under siege. Reading books like Klein's *This Changes Everything,* and *Merchants of Doubt,* by Naomi Oreskes and Erik M. Conway, offered me new insights into how science, politicians, and society all react to change. This research gave me a new perspective.

THE THINK TANK FROM ALPHA CENTAURI

If 50 million people say a foolish thing, it is still a foolish thing.

—*Anatole France*

While reading several books about environmental concerns of the past 60 years or so, I was impressed at how influential policy-making institutes, or *think tanks*, were in determining public attitudes and opinions, and in dictating political actions at the highest levels. By definition, a think tank is a body of experts providing advice and ideas on specific political or economic problems. They are frequently referred to as policy or research institutes and are generally created to market their ideas and solutions for a set of problems. While some think tanks are non-profit, many receive donations from corporations, individuals, and even from the federal government. There are approximately 2,000 think tanks in this country and at least twice that many worldwide. Some of the more influential and well-known include the Brookings Institute, Family Kaiser Foundation, Human Rights Watch, Heritage Foundation, and Earth Institute. Understandably, their ideas and proposals tend to favor their creators and financial backers, but most maintain high credibility with noted experts in the area of concern. How they have promoted public welfare—and, at times, obfuscated the issues for special economic interests—is both a fascinating and convoluted story. A few vignettes will help illustrate the roles they have played.

By the mid-1980s, the causes and consequences of acid rain were generally accepted by most scientists. But the Cato Institute asserted that the causes were not certain and any attempt to decrease acid rain would be too expensive. Furthermore, Edward Krug, of the Connecticut Agricultural Research Station, argued that acidification of the soil was natural, and not primarily due to acid rain. Krug's idea was published in *Policy Review,* by the Hoover Institution. The result of these "thoughts" was to delay the control of sulfates being dumped into the atmosphere. In 1994, the Marshall Institute, through a report authored by Fred Seitz, argued that the ozone hole predated the presence of chlorofluorocarbons and, furthermore, that CFCs couldn't reach the stratosphere. The Heritage Foundation, founded in 1973, depicted ozone depletion as a natural phenomenon exploited by the science community to garner money for research. Perhaps some of the most egregious ideas from think tanks were related to the tobacco industry's efforts to protect and promote the sale of their products.

In 1958, the tobacco industry founded the Tobacco Institute (TI) to communicate the industry's point of view on potential health-related problems. The institute cast doubt on the hazards of secondhand smoke through a think tank, the Alexis de Tocqueville Institution. It is apparent that think tanks have played a role in forming policies related to the tobacco industry, acid rain, the ozone hole problem and, later, climate change. The tactics of minimizing the problems and questioning the science of cause and effect have prolonged the resolution for these challenges. Think tanks have infiltrated the higher levels of government to influence the regulation of industry. Oh, the thoughts they can think!

I confess that my understanding of how think tanks influence government regulations was very sketchy. I was naïve and oblivious to the nuances of the legal process. In my world, scientists ruled. But in realpolitik, they were just players. I admit I was both intrigued and dismayed with the role think tanks have played in our culture. But what could I do about it? This quandary induced me to take a novel approach. I realized I could think! At least, I was pretty sure I could. Given adequate motivation and a favorable setting, I could do at least as well as the Scarecrow in *The Wizard of Oz*. I could tell you why the oceans near the shore. I could think of things I'd never thunk before. And then I'd sit right down and think some more. Furthermore, I had several friends who could think! Why couldn't we start our own think tank? I could buy some coffee and donuts, and rent the conference room at the nearby Hampton Inn. Our thoughts might be just as valuable as those of the Heritage Foundation—maybe even better. I was pretty excited about the idea for a few minutes. But then reality set in. How would our wonderful thoughts get promoted? How could the public benefit if they never found out about them? And how would our supporters materialize and who would pay for us to think? Bummer! For the immediate future, a real functionable think tank seemed unachievable. Maybe I could try another avenue.

Viewing my situation from a detached perspective was helpful. If creating a real live think tank was off the table, perhaps there were other options? Maybe I could create a hypothetical think tank. That way, I could mentally evaluate the thoughts without doing all the legwork. It would be just a mind game, and who knows where it would lead. The hooker, of course, was that any think tank on earth, real or imaginary, would reflect the views and biases of their origin. An extraterrestrial source might be best, to avoid the pit falls of self-interest. Something like an intra-galactic think tank, that's the ticket. Anybody who believes the direction of this chronicle is too far *out there* may find this a good time to abandon ship, find something else to read—or maybe go to a movie. But let me just remind you of my objective, which is to appreciate the role that think tanks and private interests have played in shaping economic and environmental policies in the past, and how they are likely to continue doing so. There are tiny truths that define our day-to-day lives. But there are greater truths that shape the destiny of Humankind—these are the ones I'm talking about.

Here's what I came up with. A panel of four climate experts from Alpha Centauri would form the core group. In addition, four more panel members would be chosen from the Milky Way, based on their expertise in a relevant scientific specialty such as physics or biology. No one chosen would have a direct connection with a fossil fuel company or any intragalactic transportation industry. All members would receive an adequate stipend from the Alpha Centauri Governmental Council for Environmental Studies. All financial transactions would be transparent; any money exchange with outsiders would be grounds for dismissal from the think tank. Panel members would garner a significant amount of prestige from the science community. But nobody could expect to get rich. The think tank had a specific mission: determine the current environmental and climate trends on the Planet Earth, and make recommendations to the UN and IPCC to assure survival and welfare of Homo sapiens for at least 1,000 years. They would have a full year (earth time) to make a final report, but were expected to give a formal progress report at six months. As the chief architect for this panel, I would initially meet with the panel members to answer any procedural questions and get them started in the right direction. I would also confer with them on a monthly basis, making myself available to help allay any friction or disputes among members. We all know how these problems can interfere with progress and the ultimate successful completion of a mission. Even though four of the panel members were from Alpha Centauri, many of the meetings and activities would take place on earth, since that was at the center of their investigation.

I scheduled our first meeting outdoors in the Greenbrier Cove, near the ranger station, for convenience and to let the panel members appreciate the natural environment of the Great Smoky Mountains National Park, the most visited park in the country, and the one with its oldest mountains. All panel members were fluent in English and had distinguished themselves by some research or scientific achievement. The Alpha Centauri panelists would spend the first month learning about earth's history, including cultural differences, energy development, economy, industry, and major military conflicts. Then they would get down to business.

As I met with the panel for the first time, it was easy to spot the members from Alpha Centauri; they all had the characteristic elongated cranium and prominent acoustic receptors on the side, a little higher and more prominent than on Homo sapiens. One of the four appeared to be somewhat older and taller than the other three. I guessed he was their coordinator. There was a heavy-set humanoid that appeared to be from Eastern Europe; I'm guessing Russia based on his accent. But there's no way to be certain. Next to him was a humanoid with the facial features of a Native American, but he said almost nothing so this made identification difficult. Behind him stood another humanoid that appeared to be Asian. His face looked familiar, but I couldn't place where I had seen it. The last panel member was a somewhat bizarre looking creature, I'm guessing from the outer Sagittarius spiral arm of the galaxy. He appeared uncomfortable and a little out of place, but I tried not to pre-judge anyone. You never know. As I explained the itinerary and mission of the panel, I reminded them to avoid jumping to judgments based on reading reports on various issues, even if it seemed to be from a reliable source. The Sagittarius creature was incredulous. He wanted me to give an example of how a noteworthy scientist might give a report that is false or misleading. So, I relayed the Story of Rachael Carson and the banning of DDT. In *Silent Spring,* she raised serious questions about the chemical DDT used to control mosquitoes and other insects in the 1940s – 1960s. Carson noted the pesticides tended to get incorporated in the food chain, causing a significant drop in the numbers of local fish and bird populations, including the bald eagle. Carson also raised the possibility that DDT might act as a carcinogen in humans or other mammals who ingested animals lower on the food chain with DDT in their tissues. Whereas she incurred the wrath and criticism of many, especially from the chemical industries that profited from the sale of pesticides, Carson also garnered respect from many officials, including President John F. Kennedy.

In the early '60s, Kennedy requested that the PSAC (President's Science Advisory Committee) advise him on the matter. Despite the difficulty of the task, PSAC came to a clear conclusion: it was time to restrict the use of DDT due to its deleterious effects on wildlife. In 1970, the Environmental Protection Agency (EPA) was created and, in 1972, ten years after *Silent Spring* was published, the use of DDT was banned in the U.S. However, there was reasonable doubt as to its safety. Although Carson died in 1964, she became symbolic of the environmental movement and a hero to many; and her death didn't stop revisionist attacks years later.

In 2007, the *San Francisco Examiner* alleged, "Carson was wrong and millions of people continue to pay the price." A writer associated with the Hoover Institution asserted, "There has not been a mass murderer executed in the past half-century who has been responsible for as many deaths of human beings as the sainted Rachel Carson." A number of websites echo these claims. How could this be? While it is true many deaths caused by malaria continued after the banning of DDT in developing countries, they were not primarily due to the lack of DDT. Use of DDT in this country peaked in 1959, 13 years before it was banned. That is because mosquitoes were developing resistance well before the ban. A similar problem was developing overseas at the same time. Resistance to DDT was a universal problem and the EPA had no jurisdiction in other countries. It is noteworthy that other factors were extremely important in the spread of disease.

More than 22,000 workers died of malaria and yellow fever between 1882 and 1889 in Panama, during Ferdinand de Lesseps's failed attempt to build a canal. In 1904, the U.S. government took over and made insect control a priority. They drained swamps and standing water and fumigated the buildings. Between 1906 and 1914, there was only one reported death from yellow fever and the overall death rate dropped dramatically—all before the use of DDT.

I could go on, but I felt the Sagittarian got the point. I merely wanted to alert the panel members to the nuances of interpreting pre-existing documents. I thought it was unnecessary to explain how women with higher serum levels of DDT and its metabolites were five times as likely to develop breast cancer; they would come across that in their reviews. But now the "Russian" introduced a new controversy. He was aware that former Vice President Al Gore had given a big boost to the credibility of the global warming theory based on greenhouses gases in his book, *An Inconvenient Truth,* and documentary film by the same name, both released in 2006. He also knew that Gore had studied under Roger Revelle at Harvard in the 1960s and that Revelle was the primary inspiration for his advocacy.

Unfortunately, the Russian claimed that Revelle had changed his opinion on global warming around 1990, completely undermining Gore's credibility. The basis for that claim was a paper published in 1991 entitled, "What To Do about Greenhouse Warming: Look Before You Leap." The primary author was S. Fred Singer; Revelle was listed second, and Chauncey Starr third. The paper downplayed the possibility of future warming and seemed to contradict Revelle's earlier assertions. On the surface, it appeared the Russian had a good point. Revelle's role in producing this paper, however, is controversial. According to the authors of *Merchants of Doubt,* Revelle's suggestions for changes did not prevail. The paper published in April 1991 contradicted Revelle's views expressed in a November 1990 meeting, that warming in the next century would be between two and five degrees centigrade. Revelle suffered a major heart attack in February 1990 and was generally in poor health during the editing process. We will never know what he thought about the paper released in April 1991 because, in July 1991, he suffered a second heart attack, this one fatal. The Revelle family felt that his name was being used unfairly to undermine Al Gore. On September 3, 1992 an article by George Will in the Washington Post, *Al Gore's Green Guilt"* attacked Gore's credibility. Revelle's daughter, Carolyn Hufbauer, wrote an op-ed refuting Will's attacks. Two of Revelle's esteemed colleagues, Walter Munk and Edward Frieman, wrote a letter to *Cosmos* claiming his views were misrepresented. *Cosmos* refused to publish it. I sensed the Russian was somewhat angry but, at the same time, seemed to back off a bit. I decided that was an adequate introduction on my part. They were all capable of dealing with conflict and making up their own minds. That was the whole idea. I would be meeting with them again in just a month or so anyway.

I was exhausted after this meeting. I had to continuously remind myself this was all a mind game. But somehow my autonomic nervous system interpreted the proceedings as a real event. I felt antsy and a little flaked out. What I needed was a pleasant diversion to take my mind off this issue. My wife had the perfect solution. Why not visit Cades Cove?

CADES COVE

Who is more to be pitied, a writer bound and gagged by policemen or one living in perfect freedom who has nothing more to say?

—Kurt Vonnegut

Cades Cove is arguably the best known and most visited section of the Great Smoky Mountains National Park. Like the Greenbrier section, it was settled in the early 19th century by pioneers seeking a better life who were willing to brave the elements of nature and deal with the local indigenous population of Cherokee. It has no direct connection with Greenbrier Cove, and is about an hour's drive to the west at the opposite end of the park. However, there are a number of striking parallels and contrasts in their respective stories of development.

Unlike Greenbrier, Cades Cove is relatively flat with an average elevation of about 1,750 feet, but is also completely surrounded by mountains with some rising to over 5,000 feet. Eighteen streams crisscross the cove, and the surrounding mountains receive the country's highest annual rainfall outside of the Pacific Northwest. The resulting cove hardwood forest contains more than 100 native trees and a biological diversity unmatched elsewhere in the U.S. The Cherokee frequently used the cove for hunting, with temporary settlements and multiple trails predating the white settlers. The Cherokee name for the cove was Tsiyahi or otter place. But the white settlers referred to it as Cades Cove after Chief Kade. Although geographic isolation and the Native Americans' threat were intimidating to the early white settlers, John and Lucretia Oliver from Carter County, Tennessee, were actually saved from starvation during their first winter, 1818 – 1819, when the local Cherokee took pity on them and gave them dried pumpkin to eat. Had the Cherokee known then that only 20 years later they would be forcibly evacuated to Oklahoma during the infamous Trail of Tears, they might have acted otherwise. Ironically, John Oliver was among the local militia charged with rounding up the remaining Cherokee in 1838 for their removal. In 1821, the Olivers' former neighbors, Joshua Jobe and several family members, including four-year-old Abraham, also moved to Cades Cove. After encouraging the Olivers to move in 1818, Joshua was able to appease Lucretia's anger by gifting the Olivers two milk cows. Abraham Jobe would later go on to be a prominent East Tennessee physician, attending to President Andrew Johnson on his deathbed.

Peter and Catherine Cable bought land in Cades Cove in 1825 and moved shortly thereafter from Pennsylvania. Peter, by all accounts, was an innovative genius who supervised construction of a series of dikes, sluices, and canals to drain the swampy regions and provide power for gristmills. He also designed and made a number of tools for local farmers. Many of the cove's buildings show evidence of his craftmanship. Perhaps the cove's most noted entrepreneur, however, was Daniel D. Foute, who built the Cades Cove Bloomery Forge on Forge Creek in 1827, thus opening the doors to the Industrial Age. Besides making a variety of tools, the forge produced a highly accurate short-range flintlock rifle. This was an extraordinary feat at the time and essential to the mountain people for protection, survival, and feeding their families. Apparently, the sound from the forge had the added unexpected benefit of scaring all of the wolves away from the farmlands. Although the maximum population of Cades Cove was only about 700, as opposed to 1,000 in Greenbrier, it would seem there was a high degree of sophistication. For example, in 1850, there was quite a variety of specialized occupations. In addition to farmers, millers, and blacksmiths, the cove housed five carpenters from Holland, several mechanics from England, a lawyer from Pennsylvania, a doctor, and a boatswain. This diversity, along with the rich farmland and plentiful game, helped ensure the settlers would not lack basic necessities. In addition, the natural abundance of Panax quinquefolium, or ginseng, provided a cash crop greater than the chestnut. A pound would bring $0.71 in 1822, $1.04 in 1871, and $5.38 in 1901.

During the Civil War, the vast majority of the Cades Cove residents sided with the Union, as did Knoxville, and most of East Tennessee. One underlying reason may have been that the North-South orientation of the Tennessee Valley made a geographic connection of the area more likely with eastern Pennsylvania and New York than with the strongly Confederate-allied North Carolina. Furthermore, Maryville College, founded in 1819 as a seminary, became a center for free thought and abolition, advocating the virtues of the anti-slavery movement. Though strongly unified, this political anomaly did lead to some conflicts within the cove. Intermittent harassment and theft by Confederate raiders from North Carolina became fairly common as the war progressed. But the cove residents organized under the leadership of Russell Gregory, one of their most famous and beloved residents, to anticipate and defend against these raids. In 1864, a raid that included Gregory's own son, Charles, was successfully thwarted when his sister purposefully detained him outside the cove, allowing time to prepare. Two weeks later, however, some of the raiders slipped into the cove at night and murdered Gregory as he got out of bed. His martyrdom outraged the community and served to rally the residents against the Confederate invaders. Russell Gregory became a local legend. Gregory Bald, elevation 4,948 feet, located a few miles southwest of Cades Cove, was named in his honor.

Equally appalling was the fate of Daniel Davis Foute, the industrialist who started the forge in 1827 and did much to develop early roads and commerce in East Tennessee. Unlike most East Tennessee residents, Foute was a Confederate sympathizer. At the close of the war in 1865, he was dragged from sickbed in Cades Cove and jailed in Knoxville. He died an indigent shortly thereafter at the nearby home of his daughter.

After the Civil War, the population dropped significantly and commerce slowed in Cades Cove until the late 1800s, as it did elsewhere. During this time frame, William Howell Oliver (1857 – 1940), grandson of the original settler John Oliver, served as minister of Cades Cove Primitive Baptist Church founded in 1827. Several other Baptist and Methodist churches came later—four altogether. These churches helped foster a law-abiding atmosphere where issues like public intoxication, disorderly conduct, and adultery were minimized by the churches' active role in the community. On the other hand, Chestnut Flats was a section on the southwest edge of the cove that developed a reputation for distilling brandy and moonshine, especially after the war. George Powell and Sam Burchfield were the mainstays, but many families drifted in and out. Predictably, this area became infested with other activities like gambling and prostitution.

Unfortunately, many people have created their image of mountain folks in Tennessee based on tales and folklore of places like Chestnut Flats. This is both unfair and misleading. More typical were the law-abiding church attending citizens of Cades Cove proper. Although domestic fights and feuding between families did occasionally occur, it never degenerated to the level of the Hatfields and McCoys of West Virginia and Kentucky. When discussions of creating a national park began in the mid-1920s, the Cades Cove residents faced the same crisis as the residents of Greenbrier Cove. In 1926, both U.S. Senator Lawrence C. Tyson and Tennessee Governor Austin Peay openly reassured the cove residents that their homes would not be taken from

them. The final bill passed by Congress in 1927, however, inval-
idated these promises. A leader in the fight to save their homes
in Cades Cove was John W. Oliver, great-grandson of the settler
John Oliver. Despite a hard-fought legal battle, by 1932 the cove
residents realized all hope of keeping their homes was lost. As
a concession, some residents were granted the right to sell their
farms and then lease them from the government in order to live
the remainder of their lives in the cove, if they so desired. The
last person living in Cades Cove was Kermit Caughron, who died
April 5, 1999, after residing there for 86 years.

My fascination with Cades Cove was piqued at an early
age. I recall riding around the 11-mile loop that circumscribes
the cove with my family in the early '60s. Just think, we were
told, some of the original settlers are still living here. I could only
imagine Snuffy Smith and Maw eking out a meager existence
with primitive tools and little knowledge of the outside world.
Understandably, my respect and admiration for these hardy souls
soared dramatically as I gained an appreciation of the obstacles
they faced and what they accomplished. How many people, given
the same challenge today, would do as well? How many would
even survive?

Recently I was reminded of a Hollywood movie, *A Walk in
the Spring Rain,* which was shot primarily in Cades Cove and
starred Anthony Quinn and Ingrid Bergman. It was filmed in 1969
and released in 1970. I made a point to view the film recently to
expand my appreciation of the area. The plot is based around a
New York professor, Roger Meredith (Fritz Weaver) and his wife,
Libby (Ingrid Bergman) who come to Cades Cove for a sabbatical.
While staying in this rustic setting, Libby has a brief affair with
Will Cade (Anthony Quinn), the property manager and mountain
man par excellence. Got it? That's all right, neither did I. The
movie was not a commercial success, and I can't heartily recommend it to any average moviegoer. There are two categories of
viewers, however, who might find it worthwhile. The first would

be anyone who's familiar with the Cades Cove and Gatlinburg area and wants to see major Hollywood stars in their hometown or stomping grounds. The other would be people obsessed with Ingrid Bergman. This caught me on both counts. The film opens with some scenes ostensibly in New York, followed by some shots allegedly at the professor's university. However, I knew better. In the background of this scene was Ayers Hall, a historic fixture on the hilltop of the University of Tennessee. I had many classes, including calculus and advanced differential equations, in that building. In another scene, Libby and Roger are seen doing Gatlinburg à la 1969. If you can remember how the tourist town looked 50-odd years ago, these scenes will in all probability elicit a nostalgic déjà vu. But my favorite scene is when Libby walks down the country road in Cades Cove dressed in New York high fashion. Her radiant glow makes even the phenomenal beauty of the cove seem ho-hum. This brings up the other major reason someone might want to see the movie: seeing Ingrid Bergman herself. Bergman is, in my opinion, the greatest and most beau-tiful actress of all time. Scarlett Johansson, Meryl Streep, and Elizabeth Taylor, all rolled up in one. Bergman's beauty, grace, and acting skills suggest she originated in a celestial paradise far away and was merely "loaned" to earthlings for a finite number of years. I don't know how else to explain it. It did occur to me that readers under the tender age of 40 might not remember too much about Ms. Bergman, unless they've seen her unforgettable role in *Casablanca*. She is best known for her roles in *Casablanca* (1942) and *Notorious* (1946), but won Academy Awards for *Gaslight* (1945) *Anastasia* (1957), *Autumn Sonata* (1979) and *Murder on the Orient Express* (1975). She was born August 29, 1915, in Stockholm, Sweden, and after a brief film career in Sweden she moved to Hollywood where her career exploded. She died in London on August 29, 1982, 67 years to the day after birth. It is my hope that perhaps this is all a big mix-up and maybe she merely got recalled to her celestial place of origin. If that's true we may be blessed with her re-appearance at some later time.

By far the best way to experience the essence of Cades Cove is to travel around it on the perimeter road. It is open to traffic year-round, weather permitting, from sunrise to sunset except on Wednesdays when it is closed to all motor vehicles. This allows hikers, runners, and cyclists to enjoy the 11-mile excursion without the nuisance of motor traffic. I have completed this scenic journey four or five times. My favorite method of travel is cycling. This allows a pleasant trip in a few hours, giving ample time to espy wildlife (it is one of the most probable places in the park to see a black bear) without overtaxing your physical endurance. The panoramic vista is extraordinary year-round, but I am especially enamored by the changing colors of foliage in spring and autumn.

After several cancellations due to weather and personal conflicts, I finally found time for a bike trip in late spring 2020. I inspected my 15-year-old 24-speed mountain bike, making sure the tires were inflated before I artfully placed it in my Outback Subaru. This required me to fold down the back seats and contort the handlebars before it would fit. I then headed west on U.S. 321 for the roughly 60-minute drive to Cades Cove. Being stuck behind a camper going 30 miles per hour on Little River Road, however, assured it would take more than an hour. At the Cades Cove parking area, I backed into a parking slip. I painstakingly delivered the bike from its contorted position out the rear door. It seemed none the worse for wear except that, on checking the brakes, I discovered the brake cable on the front wheel had come loose from its metal casing and the bracket slightly bent. I suppose this was a complication of the extraction process. This wasn't a deal breaker, though. The rear brake worked just fine and I wouldn't be travelling at high speeds.

I slowly cycled to the information station so I could purchase a simple map of the trails and roads of the cove. That's when I noticed most everyone wore a face mask, for protection from the COVID-19 virus. So, I returned to the car to don my mask. I then headed west and hit the Loop Road at 8:30 a.m. Vehicular traffic was already an issue, requiring me to be on continual outlook for an approaching car or truck. As it were, however, they were moving at a snail's pace and I was just as likely to pass by them as vice versa. Had I made my trip on a Wednesday, I could have avoided this problem altogether, but that didn't fit with my personal schedule. No biggie.

Within the first five minutes, I observed some wild turkeys and white-tailed deer. The greatest thrill, however, was to see Ursus americanus ambling in the nearby fields or woods. Several signs with pictures resembling Yogi or Boo-Boo reminded visitors of a Donation Box and admonished them for throwing food items. At least twice I stopped alongside a group of cars pulled over for such a glimpse. Once, I did see a dark, four-legged, bear-like creature moving slowly in the distance blackberry bushes and having breakfast. But the visual was not very impressive.

Eventually, I became more interested in observing another ubiquitous species: Homo sapiens. One fairly obese male specimen had a camera set up on a tripod, presumably to catch Ursus americanus in its natural habitat. He was non-hostile and quite engaging. They seemed, for the most part, to travel in family units of four of five and showed great excitement every time someone had a possible bear sighting. I strained to see what one male claimed was a bear behind a sizeable bush about 200 yards away. But I felt more in sympathy with his female companion who exclaimed, "I'm calling it a bear stump." Traveling on from there, I was passed by a female Homo sapiens driving a late model compact car with a New York license plate. I assumed New York was her preferred habitat. As she passed, she smiled and said, "Hello" and I responded, "Good morning." I was about to ask her how she liked Cades Cove and if she had ever seen Ursus americanus in her natural habitat. But, in 30 seconds, she had moved on, never to be seen again. Yes, the American black bear is truly a fascinating species, but no one can outdo Homo sapiens in its mysterious behavior patterns and general intrigue.

A little further along, a middle-aged female and a much younger, somewhat overweight male passed by me. A good guess was that he was her offspring but, with Homo sapiens, you can never quite be sure about the relationship. I'm guessing the female was 20 years my junior. She was well tattooed and slightly withered but still vigorous as evidenced by her athletic activity. To be friendly I asked them if they knew what the beautiful purple flowers on either side of the road were called. Automatically, as if programmed for this question, she rattled off a flower name unfamiliar to me. I don't remember what she said, but I was impressed. Perhaps I could ask the rangers later. A little over halfway around the 11-mile loop, I was about ready to conclude that my trip was not too exciting. But then I arrived at the Cable Mill area. Peter Cable settled in the area in the 1820s, and John Cable in the 1860s. They were the innovative settlers mentioned earlier who played a critical role in the Cove's development. John Cable's homesite, in addition to his well-constructed house, includes a milldam and flume, gristmill, smokehouse, corn crib, cane mill, and sorghum furnace. These well-preserved feats of engineering are easy to access by the curious visitor. But what excited me most of all was an information sign, "Cable Mill Area Solar Power System," 50 yards from the visitor center.

Apparently, in 2018, the park system installed about 2,438 square feet of solar panels to supply the energy needs of the entire Cable Mill area, including the visitor center. As a result of this endeavor, the park saves the use of 4,000 gallons of propane a year with an annual cost savings of about $14,4000. As an added bonus, this has resulted in an annual reduction of CO_2 emissions totaling about 23 metric tons. It was also noted that Clingmans Dome, Sugarlands Visitor Center, and the Mt. Sterling Radio Tower had similar installations. My first impression was that the installation was inappropriate in this historic setting, as it had nothing to do with the pioneer lifestyle of the Cables or other settlers of Cades Cove. But then I got it. The early settlers were innovative and efficient. They tried to get the maximum from nature's resources and abhorred waste. If John Cable were alive today, I'm sure he would applaud this energy source. Far from distressing me, this sign brought a smile to my face. Not only is the park service making a relevant statement in a historical setting, but they also spend taxpayers' money more efficiently.

Delighted with my discovery, I left the Cable Mill area and headed east on Loop Road to complete the last four miles or so. This took me past the Dan Lawson homestead, the Tipton house, and the Carter Shields cabin—all historic buildings reflecting the rustic setting of the Cove in the 1800s. But shortly past the Carter Shields cabin, I noted five cars stopped in the road. This was not a designated pull over site, so I knew there must have been a bear sighting. Seeing me perplexed, a passenger pointed to the woods on the left. I could now clearly see a massive black ball of animated fur protruding from behind a fallen tree about 60 feet away. At one point the bear stood up, revealing his entire size. I won't give a size estimate except to say that he seemed a good bit bigger than me. I could clearly see two individual bears—perhaps mates, or mother and offspring, or playmates. They seemed to be tumbling around. I was the only one not seated in a car, but I wasn't freaked out. In the rare event one made an aggressive move in my direction, someone would surely come to the aid of an elderly cyclist. Wouldn't they?

After taking a few quick photos, I began to get antsy so I moved on. This event greatly added to my excitement and satisfaction. I would now have a few stories to tell. About 10 minutes after this encounter, I experienced another challenge. While downshifting to a lower gear as I struggled up a hill, I noted a sudden inability to pedal the bike. The chain popped off the gear mechanism and was dangling helplessly. This is really no big deal to an experienced mountain biker, but somewhat of bummer for a recreational biker like me. I decided to get off and walk the bike for a while. Fortunately, I estimated I was no more than two miles from completing the loop, and I was a good walker. But, all of a sudden, I realized there were no cars or bikers anywhere around me. What if I encountered more specimens of Ursus americanus? Of course, as I've noted elsewhere, bears, generally speaking, are not a big threat if you use common sense. Still, not only are they bigger and stronger than I, but they can also easily outrun, not to mention out climb, me. So, I was delighted when, about five minutes later, I met a middle-aged man in his pickup truck. "Need any help?" he asked. After first declining help, I admitted it would be nice if he could help me re-set the chain on the gear mechanism. This was easily accomplished when he pushed the rear derailleur down, allowing enough slack in the chain for me to easily place it back on the correct gear. Then he raised the derailleur, causing the chain to fit snugly in place. I thanked him heartily and went on my merry way.

This episode reinforced my faith in the good will of Homo sapiens. They seem to be at least as pleasant as Ursus americanus, especially on a one-on-one encounter. From there, I completed the loop in two hours without further incident, and returned to my parked car at 10:20 a.m. Not bad considering my frequent stops and leisurely pace. I made it home in about one hour and 15 minutes, which included a stop at Food City. Back at my cabin, I delivered the bike once again from my Subaru's rear door and wheeled it into the garage. I now had a better opportunity to examine the damaged front wheel brake. By comparing the cable mechanism on the front wheel with that on the back, I was able to successfully replace the cable in its metal casing, and bend the metal bracket more or less to its original shape with a pair of pliers. Then I tested it out. Seemed to work just fine. So, I could happily conclude that my Cades Cove tour was worthwhile. I gained a historical perspective of how the early settlers met their energy and dietary needs. I had an encounter of the third kind with an American black bear or three, and several encounters with Homo sapiens. I acquired an enhanced appreciation for the innovative spirit and good will of Homo sapiens. But I will continue to hold in awe the natural beauty and physical prowess of Ursus americanus.

TROUBLES IN GREENBRIER

Prejudice is a raft onto which the shipwrecked mind clambers and paddles to safety.

—Ben Hecht

The brief tour of Cades Cove helped restore my spiritual energy and refocus my personal goals. At the same time, I felt a strong urge to return to Greenbrier Cove, my home base. There seemed to be some unfinished business, but the exact nature of that business had not crystalized in my mind. I decided to hike the Porters Creek Trail to view the wildflowers and clear my head. Porters Trail begins about four miles from the Greenbrier entrance to the park on U.S. 321. At about one mile, it passes by the old John Messer farm site with a barn built in 1875 by John Whaley. Adjacent to the barn is a cabin built by the Smoky Mountains Hiking Club in the 1930s. At two miles, the Fern Branch Falls will be visible on the left. Wildflowers—bloodroot, hepaticas, phacelia, trillium, wild geranium, blue phlox, and dwarf ginseng, among others—attract hikers from many other states and countries during the spring months.

This four-mile round trip moderate trail was enough for me. On the way back to my cabin, I stopped to rest at the junction of Porters Creek and the Middle Prong of the Little Pigeon River. It was near this site that James and Kimsey Whaley converted the old Greenbrier schoolhouse into the LeConte Hotel in 1925. The hotel was abandoned in 1935 with the creation of the park. But, at $1.75 per night, it must have had the most awesome views for the money that could be found. Such a setting is conducive to finding peace, but that doesn't necessarily mean it comes easily. To a parent, peace may mean resolving underlying conflicts with children. To an artist, it may mean gaining respect and understanding for one's works. For all who labor, peace might mean that they gain acknowledgement and satisfaction from their efforts. Above all, most people want to be reassured later in life that they have made a difference. Or, as American poet Diane Ackerman once said, "I don't want to get to the end of my life and find that I have lived the length of it. I want to have lived the width of it as well."

Staring at the tumbling water induced a hypnotic trance. It was only then that the nature of my unfinished business resurfaced. My mind game with the think tank from Alpha Centauri had raised some unresolved dilemmas. Maybe my Personal Legend was to somehow resolve those conflicts. Again, viewing myself from a detached perspective, I imagined the following scenario: The eight-member think tank was holding a follow-up meeting on the banks of the Little Pigeon River near the site of the old LeConte Hotel one month after their inaugural meeting. The coordinator from Alpha Centauri acknowledged my presence and began eliciting feedback from the other members. The Sagittarius native was the first to report. He spoke slowly with poise and confidence, suggesting he had spent considerable time and energy on his mission. His main focus was to review the IPCC reports and minutes—created in 1988 by the United Nations and the World Meteorological Organization (WMO)— to examine the causes and significance of climate change. He was impressed that many of the world's top climate scientists were meticulously collecting data and offering credible theories for the climate variations. He also noted that research by Ben Santer at Lawrence Livermore National Laboratory used sophisticated statistical methods to detect the anthropogenic fingerprint on the current global warming trend. The takeaway message of the Sagittarius native was clear and credible. Global warming was real and traceable to human activities. No one could have said it better.

The next report came from an Alpha Centauri panel member. His focus was to review possible technological options to help prevent the onset of man-made warming. One plan was to create machines that could suck CO_2 from the atmosphere to decrease its greenhouse effect. Another techno fix proposal was to decrease the heat form the sun by spraying stratospheric sulfate aerosols into the atmosphere to reflect sunlight, precisely what occurs after volcanic eruptions. This technique known as solar radiation management (SRM) has garnered support from billionaires Richard Branson and Bill Gates. Other proposals were merely to aggressively plant more trees and vegetation to assist in decreasing greenhouse gases. His report was thorough and professional. But at the same time, he was not very optimistic about any of these options. "The bottom line," he said, "is that these options are not cost-effective compared to the simple option of decreasing our consumption of fossil fuels."

The next presenter was the Native American. His news was not good at all. He was a little reserved and tentative at first, but his message was arguably one of the most important. "The problems caused by greenhouse gases could be even worse than some earlier predictions from the IPCC. The earth's oceans have served as sort of a temperature moderator, absorbing a lot of excess atmospheric heat. This explains, in part, the lack of a good correlation between rising atmospheric carbon dioxide levels and global temperatures during the middle part of the 20th century. As the ocean heats up, however, this moderating effect will diminish and allow for more warming. Furthermore," he argued, "several outside issues could cause an acceleration of the problem. As the Permafrost in northern Canada and Siberia melts, an abundance of carbon dioxide trapped in the frozen organic matter of the tundra will be released. The exact quantity is very difficult to predict. At the same time, as the glaciers of the two poles and Greenland melt, the reflective power of the earth's ice and snow will diminish proportionately. Known as the albedo effect, this phenomenon assured that as a warmer climate melts ice, a feedback loop would create even more warming." The speaker admitted that quantifying these effects was very difficult, but there seemed no way to deny their existence. He was so morose and emotional over his message that I felt sorry for him. He barely managed to complete his presentation without losing his composure.

As the other panel members completed their presentations on related topics, I noticed the Russian panel member sitting on a rock close to the river on my left. He patiently waited for his turn to speak, but seemed to become increasingly restless and agitated as each speaker made his case. His body language suggested he was not pleased with the way things were going. Finally, as the coordinator gave him the nod to proceed, he stood up and addressed the panel. I distinctly remember he wore a heavy, wool, purple shirt, not made anywhere around here. His ruddy complexion was a good match. The combination of his attire, complexion, and Russian accent made him stand out from the others. There was also something very sinister about his appearance, but I did my best not to prejudge him or anyone else. Sadly, his opening comments affirmed my worst fears. After barely acknowledging the existence of the other panelists, the Russian attempted to undermine their conclusions. "A number of famous scientists had examined these theories and found them full of holes," he said. "These were mostly famous physicists, who had played an important role in WW II and the Cold War with their work on the atomic bomb, satellite technology, and the Strategic Defense Initiative (SDI), also known as Star Wars, under the Reagan Administration—namely Fred Seitz, Fred

Singer, William Nirenberg, and Robert Jastrow. All these scientists had distinguished themselves in the world of physics and had served as science advisors and consultants at the highest levels. Their primary contribution was to raise serious doubt about the theory of global warming due to greenhouse gases. They couldn't disprove it, but argued that it didn't make sense to spend major resources for a problem that might not exist." So, this was the card the Russian was playing: doubt and uncertainty made actions unwarranted. He paused briefly after this prelude to feel out his audience.

I took the opportunity to make a rebuttal. "Yes," I said, "but all these scientists were trained as physicists, and none of them had training in climate science. Furthermore, despite their noted accomplishments, they did relatively little original research after around 1970. Their main role seemed to be to function as contrarians to the mainstream scientists. Weren't these the same scientists, some of whom denied the scientific relationship between tobacco and lung cancer, between pollution and acid rain, and between CFCs and the ozone hole? Weren't they more famous for their ability to raise doubts about climate science than for any positive contribution in that field?" I could tell my words disturbed him because his breathing became more labored. "That's ridiculous," he panted, "these guys had inside connections all the way to the White House and played a major role in setting national policies." I started to tell him that was part of our problem; instead, I decided to try another route.

"The works of the climate scientists at IPCC were all peer reviewed and accepted by the mainstream science world. Your scientists had direct connections with think tanks subsidized by the fossil fuel industry and in some cases the tobacco industry," I reminded him. I didn't know how to keep this confrontation under control, but I was in it too far to back down. Where was it leading? But now the Russian, aware of the growing tension, tried a new tactic. He wanted to know if I had read the *New York*

Times bestseller, *Unstoppable Global Warming, Every 1,500 Years,* by Fred Singer in 2007. "It reveals the fallacies of the global warming alarmist and explains why they are all wrong." He seemed confident that he had subdued me now, but he had only pushed my buttons. I had read the book several times and dissected its message. So, I was ready with a comeback. I politely but firmly offered my explanations.

The book attempted to allay the concern for recent warming due to greenhouse gases by minimizing the recent trend and suggesting historic swings in the earth's temperature were mostly due to variations in solar energy. It contained a collection of theories and statistics from various sources that, on the surface, seemed to undermine the assertions of the IPCC and other climate scientists. Whereas it raised credible concerns, it didn't seem to offer an airtight alternative that was any better. I broke the essence of the book into three general claims. First: A claim that global warming is insignificant. The foreword by Joseph L. Bast in Singer's book clearly states that there has been no warming trend in the U.S. since the 1930s. Second: Any current global warming (If it does exist) is due to variation in solar energy, not an increase in greenhouse gases. Third: Global warming (if and when it occurs) would be a good thing. Plants would grow better due to more carbon dioxide, and frigid climates could now grow crops that were previously grown in temperate climates. Flooding from rising oceans could be dealt with as it occurs. The earth has had much higher ocean levels in its history. Life goes on.

On the surface, these claims appear to undermine the mainstream climate scientists and their theories. A closer look, however, will do just the opposite. The first claim is easy to refute. No rational being can deny that the earth's surface temperatures are slowly increasing. Claims that the people recording the temperatures chose sites near cities that are somewhat above normal or didn't know what they were doing is laughable. Perhaps we can excuse the author partially. In 2007 the warming trend was statistically significant, but not to the same degree as in 2020. The second claim deserves consideration. The theory that variations in solar activity is causing climate change has some credibility. It has been around a while. Statistical evaluations by Ben Santer and others show a much stronger correlation with atmospheric carbon dioxide levels. Science is not perfection nor absolute certainty, but rather a process to offer the best explanation for observations. The greenhouse warming theory is the best fit. The third claim that the world will be better off in a warmer CO_2-rich atmosphere also deserves consideration. Certainly, it is true that some crops could be grown further north than today, like in Russia. But the decreased productivity in the tropics and temperate zones, and the vegetation losses in the same areas, would most likely outweigh the gains. Furthermore, although coastal flooding has certainly occurred in the distant past, the total vulnerable population living near oceans today is far greater. So, a rational human being cannot easily dismiss that risk. But perhaps the greatest weakness is the general random shotgun approach to denial.

Overall, the book reminds me of a humorous argument I was advised to use by a senior doctor during my anesthesiology residency. If someone falsely accused me of using and breaking their equipment, I should make the following claims: First, I never borrowed your [laryngoscope]. Second, it was broken when I got it. Third, it worked perfectly fine when I returned it. Each statement may or may not be true, but they are not mutually reinforcing arguments. The validity of the first argument raises questions about the validity of the second and third.

It was only after finishing my little presentation did I notice how outraged the Russian had become. Clearly, there was something different about the Russian compared to the other panelists. He seemed unbalanced. All panel members had been vetted for their academic and science credentials, and for any possible connections with the fossil fuel industry. Now I recalled that some

135

investigators claimed the Russian had been seen partying with OPEC officials last year in Vienna. But no financial connection was ever proved. I wish we had researched that red flag a little better. Too late for that now.

Befuddled, but not yet defeated, the Russian gave it one last try. "Numerous 'scientists' had poked holes in the theory of anthropogenic global warming," he claimed. Had I not heard of publications by Calvin Fray, Gregory Wrightstone, Rod Martin Jr., Alan Moran, and Joe Bastardi? These men and their works had proved the theory wrong and dangerous. He stood there glaring at me. Indeed, I had read all these authors. They were all intelligent people with science backgrounds, but not necessarily in climate science. For the most part, they weren't presenting original research or theories that underwent the rigorous peer-review process; they merely rehashed data that raised some important questions. Furthermore, most of these issues had been addressed by the IPCC. Giving them equal time to the real climate scientists was illogical. Although they seemed credible, their message was more one of obfuscation and confusion than of clarity and resolution. As a final blow, I averred, "They say the exact things you would expect someone hired by the fossil fuel companies would say to hide the link between their products and global warming." The Russian's rage became uncontrollable. Rushing directly at me, his outstretched arms locked with mine. In a show of strength, he slowly pushed me backward a few steps until he came to his senses. Suddenly embarrassed by his own immature behavior, he dropped his arms but continued to glare at my face. Obviously, I had hit a nerve. Only now did I realize my own vulnerability. The other seven panelists were sympathetic to my political stance, but where would their loyalty lie if a physical fight erupted? They had certainly formed some strong bonds as an elite group with a challenging mission. Even If they remained neutral, which I thought they would probably try to do, how would it pan out if the Russian and I got into it?

As calmly as possible, I tried to objectively analyze the match-up. The cold facts were not encouraging.

Purple Shirt (Russian) vs. Me

Age: About 50 vs. 71

Size: 6'2" and 220 lbs. vs. 5'10.5" and 174 lbs.

Strength: 9 out of 10 vs. 7 out of 10

Aerobic Fitness: 5 out of 10 vs. 8 out of 10

Fighting Experience: 9 out of 10 vs. 1 out of 10

I could only guess the Russian had more fighting experience than I did, given I had almost none. But I was also guessing I was a little more aerobically fit. Although he appeared to be quite strong, he definitely had a midriff bulge. In addition, I noticed a pack of Camels peeking out the top of his shirt pocket. Nevertheless, this probable advantage in aerobic fitness was almost a moot point. If he got me in a death grip in the first minute or two, it wouldn't matter; I'd be a goner. Bottom Line: Advantage, Purple Shirt. This situation caused me to rack my brain feverishly for a game plan. It was my naïve belief that even the most desperate situation had a viable adequate solution if you played your cards right. A weaker contestant might overcome his more powerful opponent with a better strategy. Even a man facing the guillotine might change his fate if he made the perfect plea at the right time. Everyone has an advantage of some type. The trick is to figure out what it is.

As an anesthesiologist I was accustomed to being a political underdog. A service-oriented professional, my work schedule was at the discretion of other physicians and patients. Being a small fish in a big pond, I had learned to play whatever cards I was dealt. But where was my ace now? Then suddenly it hit me. I did have one advantage over this more powerful player: the power of deception. The Russian was certainly a stronger, more experienced fighter. But I wasn't a pushover. Once, as a college student, a classmate tackled me to initiate a fight. He wasn't really angry or trying to injure me, he merely wanted to prove his physical dominance over a nerdy chemistry student. Men do these types of things. Within a minute, I had him crying uncle while pinned on the floor. Underestimating an opponent is a fatal mistake. Perhaps I could deceive the Russian into believing I was a pushover. While these thoughts were filling my head, I developed a plan. It was a wonderful, horrible, heavenly, diabolical plan. It rose from my very soul and permeated my entire being. Or maybe the plan was sent from above to take total control of operations? Either way, I was completely focused on the execution of the plan. There was no room left in my head for fear or doubt. It was all or none. For a few seconds we stared at each other in silence. I noticed a distraught look on the face of the coordinator from Alpha Centauri. Nobody said a word. The sound of a passing car brought me back to reality, but not totally. I was fully committed to the plan. Instead of explaining it, I will merely tell you what happened. I think you'll understand.

The Russian was standing about 10 feet in front of me. On his left were the seven other think tank members, more or less in a line. To his right was about 12 feet of open space and then a steep bank that overlooked the river four feet below. Without warning of any kind, I aggressively ran toward the Russian. But not right at him. I aimed for an imaginary point about halfway between him and the steep bank. He reacted by lunging toward me and locking arms as he had just done a minute or so before. As he pushed me backward toward the bank, I resisted, but only with about 75 percent of my strength. That was part of the plan. After about four baby steps backward, I could tell that my left foot had reached the drop off. As I carefully placed my right foot parallel to the left, I bent both my legs to about 60 degrees and simultaneously quit resisting his forward motion. When our entangled bodies formed a 45-degree angle to the earth, I pushed with both of my legs as hard as I could.

The combination of his forward momentum and the well-timed contractions of my quadriceps caused us to sail into the sky over the river. As we soared through the air, time seemed to stand still. I could clearly see his cigarettes as they fell from his pocket. And I recall how the tops of the hardwoods made a beautiful outline against the clear sky. I wondered if this would this be the final vision to register in my brain before my death, and if it would somehow be retrievable data. I wasn't necessarily panicking; I was just curious about how death worked. As I saw the water rapidly approaching, I took a big breath. He still had a death grip on me, but not really. He surely must have been more startled than I at the sudden turn of events; I had anticipated them. And then we both hit the water. Water, the miracle substance of nature. The sustainer of life and cause of many deaths. The carrier of diseases and the universal cleansing agent. The cold water of a Tennessee mountain stream in June. Advantage: me.

The shock of the cold water stunned my senses and caused a brief disorientation. But my plan was well ingrained. By swimming around and behind him, I could subdue him with a half-nelson hold while he was still in distress. One look at the Russian, however, told me that maneuver would not be necessary. He was coughing and sputtering and flailing his arms in a wild uncoordinated manner. I watched as one of the panelists from Alpha Centauri tried to offer a fallen tree branch for him to grab as he began floating downstream. I took that moment of maximum chaos to submerge and do three full breaststrokes underwater to propel me to the opposite side of the river. I then crawled—no, *slithered* would be a better word—up the riverbank and numbly walked about 30 feet until I could hide out of sight behind a massive tulip poplar tree. With one last glance I could see the Russian's purple shirt as his body floated downstream. He didn't seem to be fighting or thrashing. Exhausted, I sat on the ground, braced by the enormous tree trunk, and then sunk my head between my knees and wrapped my arms around myself for warmth. I was emotionally and physically exhausted. I must have sat there at least an hour in a semiconscious state until I had enough energy and willpower to walk back to the car. I saw no evidence of my imaginary friends.

Last Innertube Ride

*To appreciate the noble is a gain which can never
be torn from us.*

— Johann von Goethe

For several days after my imaginary confrontation with the think tank, I reviewed the details of the encounter in my mind. I was afraid to relate them to my wife, or anyone else, lest they think I was cracking up. Twice I had gone back to the site to look for evidence of a real meeting between physical beings. I found no footprints, clothing scraps, cigarettes, or other debris to suggest anything other than squirrels, chipmunks, and the usual critters had been using this picturesque piece of land by the riverside. Eventually, my anxiety decreased and I actually developed a sense of calm and well-being related to this perceived happening. Apparently, I had been using my imagination to resolve submerged conflicts. Even though I performed no useful task or solved any problems, I had researched a critical issue of our times and taken a stand. If only I could find a way to help people benefit from my insights. Perhaps that would come later. I was not overly obsessed with the prospects of death. I heeded the words of Shakespeare, "A coward dies many times before his death. The valiant never taste of death but once."

Nevertheless, I couldn't resist pondering how my last years would pan out. How many more times would I hear Brenda Lee sing "Rock Around the Christmas Tree," Van Morrison sing "Brown Eyed Girl," or Crosby, Stills and Nash sing "Teach Your Children?" Not enough, I'm afraid. My bucket list was neither extensive nor sophisticated. I did fantasize some about performing with my acoustic guitar before a live audience, but most of my aspirations were more mundane—hiking the Alum Bluff Trail to Mt. Le Conte or the Ramsey's Cascade Trail at least one more time, to start with. These were certainly doable nostalgic ventures. But then it occurred to me.

The granddaddy of all treks down memory lane would be to take a long innertube ride down the Little Pigeon River. I could put in somewhere in the park below the ranger station and ride the rapids downstream for two or three miles. I could get out somewhere past Pittman Center. This adventure would combine the thrill of shooting the rapids with the reminiscing induced by floating past all the various places I stayed by the river since 1954. I chose one of the real, ole timey innertubes from a pile of floating devices in our garage, as opposed to a faux tube meant to be a toy. After inflating and checking for leaks, I asked my wife to drive me a half mile or so into the park to a spot where lots of people splash around with their kids near the bank. As I grabbed my innertube, I told Rebecca I should be home in about two hours, but if I were not there in three to call the police to search the river. This was added in jest. A major malfunction was highly unlikely. A drowning accident could happen but I'd have to really work at it. It was late June and the water temperature was well above 60 degrees Fahrenheit—cold but tolerable. Recent rains had swollen the river enough to cover many of the rocks and help make the ride fun, but not enough to create a real danger. I wore only a bathing suit and an old pair of tennis shoes. Tied to the inflation port was a plastic sack containing a snack and some liquid refreshment. The best part was what I didn't bring: no cell phone, iPad, or other means of communication. The river further isolated me from human interference.

I now had the ideal situation, not merely for a mental trip back in time, but for decluttering my mind with whatever was clogging it up. The first clog to surface was my adverse relationship with instruction manuals. With three kids, two step-kids, and six grandkids or step-grandkids, I was a de facto expert in mechanical toy assembly. What I have learned is that the difficulty of analyzing the pedantic assembly steps, combined with the frustration of interpreting the perverse illustrations of the manual, generally far exceeds the difficulty of actually assembling the toy. A quick overview of the situation and a careful accounting of all the parts will do wonders. My experience is that if I have to actually look at the instruction manual, it doesn't bode well for an efficient assembly. A related problem concerns manuals written in four or more languages. Frequently, my obsession with trying to read the instructions in German or French far outweighs my motivation to actually assemble the toy. Therefore, I may waste 30 minutes or so before I actually get down to work. This is something, however, that I am probably going to have to work out on my own.

As I leisurely floated downstream, my innertube occasionally bumped into a river boulder, altering my direction like a metal ball in a pinball machine. I was more or less in thermodynamic equilibrium. The hot sun on my torso counterbalanced the cooling effect of the water on my lower extremities. My mind was still in decluttering mode. So, then I thought, *maybe we need more instruction manuals, not fewer.* God made Man and Woman anatomically complementary and symmetrical on a physical and emotional level. But he left no rules of engagement or detailed instructions about how to interact. He left that up to the poets, philosophers, and theologians. Maybe we could use some more detailed instructions?

But then my first important landmark loomed directly in front of me. The Conley R. Huskey Bridge that spanned the river for the two-laned highway, U.S. 321. A few hundred yards past the highway, the river splits in two, creating a sizable island of about 17 acres. Currently this real estate is the home of the Greenbrier Campground, a beautiful destination for RV owners or campers who crave enjoying nature from a rustic setting. Historically, the island was used for craft fairs and athletic competitions in the early 1900s. In 1921, it was used as a place to celebrate the opening of the Pittman Center School with music, speeches, and feasting. I chose to take the wider fork that went to the left or west side of the island. Almost immediately the Hills Creek Baptist Church mentioned earlier in this story came into view. I attended it once in 1959 and again in 2019. The church is very open and community friendly. They don't seem to mind if we occasionally use the river behind the church as a swimming hole. Note to self: remember to revisit this church in 2029.

Eventually, the two forks reunite in a beautiful setting called the Flint Rock swimming hole, named after the boulder positioned on the west bank. Here, the river suddenly becomes wider and slower moving to create a natural play area. Considered one of the top five swimming holes in the Smokies, this little paradise serves both the vacationers at the campground and those staying at the Brookside Cottages immediately downstream on the east bank. The Brookside Cottages were used as the primary site for my family's annual reunion from the mid-1980s until recently. A lot of family drama transpired at that site. In 1989, I had just separated from my first wife, Heidi. How do you explain to a six-year-old that their mommy wasn't coming to the mountains this year? But 1993 was a good year. Rebecca and I were married on the porch of the main cabin overlooking the river. Two years later, however, I was calling the police because my son had departed in the middle of the night. Too much drama! Most memories are pleasant, like of kids playing hide-and-seek in the evening with the flashlights I purchased for their cousin's birthday. But the one image that dominates my memory is of my father, solemnly sitting halfway in the water at the swimming hole in the summer of 1988. Cancer had spread throughout his body. He never complained despite what must have been horrific discomfort. His funeral would be three months later.

Passing the swimming hole, I enter a narrow straight where the current picks up speed and slings me around rocks like an agitator in a washing machine. If had paid for a ride in Dollywood, this would be where you got your money's worth. Then again, the current slows and I passed under the covered bridge not far from our cabin.

From here, the trip downstream is equivalent to traveling back in time. In another quarter-mile or so, I approached another quiet spot in the river like the swimming hole at Flint Rock. This is the area we used in the '50s, '60s, and '70s for recreation. On the right-hand side is the shallow spot where I first learned to swim in 1955. Thirty yards further is the site where my sister, Susie, was nearly swept downstream. The once quaint cabin house, Non-monotonous, that overlooked this swimming hole has been replaced with condominiums. But, surprisingly, the terrace overlooking the river where we once sat is unchanged. This property is now all privately owned and inaccessible to the public.

Despite a shallow rocky segment in the river, I continued to make good progress downstream. Occasionally, I stopped to splash cold water to cool my upper body and decrease sunburn. Finally, I reached the first cabin my parents rented in the year 1954. It has a huge screened-in porch where my siblings and I slept on cots. It doubled as a dining room and a playroom. There were no happier kids around at that time.

I continued floating downstream. The last landmark would have been an old white farmhouse another quarter-mile downstream where we stayed in 1964. Instead, two beautiful mansions now sit there, almost side-by-side. Both built in the last five years, the owners were allegedly entrepreneurs of the nouveau riche hillbilly moonshine business. Only, now it's legal. What was once the embarrassment of high society was now a major source of legitimate income. These are only places of note from my past. They all hold pleasant memories interspersed with sadness. But can they help unravel the mystery of my life's direction? That must be up to me. I now have about 15 more minutes to float downstream before it will be time to stop. My mind is still in full-on de-cluttering mode. But reality is just around the corner.

"Doctor, doctor, please help me!" the patient cried. I could tell he was in extreme pain from the look on his face. The surgery and general anesthetic had gone well, but the pain was almost unbearable. Usually, the procedures I do before surgery can minimize pain, but they are not foolproof. "Quick, get me some ten cc syringes and 0.5% Sensorcaine," I instructed the nurse. In a few minutes, I had made several injections to decrease the stabbing pain sensations. A little IV Dilaudid was a big help too. "Oh, thank you, Doc," he sighed. Beads of sweat remained on his forehead, but the crisis was averted. Was I the hero or the villain? All I could do was all I could do. These little vignettes from my four decades of medical practice had a life of their own. I really couldn't eliminate them from memory. Now, I needed to focus on the river.

One more section of the river with Class II rapids, enhanced by the recent rains, could easily capsize my little ship. So, I paddled hard to avoid the worst. But now I heard another distressed cry. Only it was more like a whimper from a frightened puppy. My gosh, I know that sound, I anguished. It was from my own child in 1989. My ex-wife had just announced to our children that we were splitting up. She was taking them to her parents in Florida. What was wrong with children these days? I mused. Why can't they deal with a little domestic instability? Surely, they understand we will still take good care of them. I will do my best to provide and see them when I can. "Oh, my God. What are we doing?" It has otherwise been a decent ride. No major mishaps, and I could feel the tension slowly leaving my body.

In a few hundred yards around the next bend, I knew a spot where it would be easy to scale the riverbank. But the decluttering process is like a mind worm. It's hard to get rid of. Now I was making the final turn into the home stretch of the mile run. I had made a good effort. I had trained hard for months with longer workout runs, sprints, and lifting weights. I had a healthy lifestyle and felt good about myself. It was now time to collect my reward. But something was terribly wrong. There, 50 yards in front of me were two runners, one from my own team nearing the finish line. It would be impossible to catch them. And now some idiot runner was trying to pass me on the outside. If he succeeded, I would be out of luck. Only the first three runners score points in a two-way meet. So, I doubled down with every last ounce of energy I had to make my legs move faster. I lunged at the finish line, barely edging out the runner to my right. In doing so I fell flat on my face. "How did you do in the mile run today?" my father asked later that evening. "Great "I said, "I got third place!" Lousy third place. I was always looking for something in which I could excel. Some skill or activity that would make me stand out in a crowd. Whether it be hula hoops, underwater swimming, or ping pong; I had felt sure there must be something. But now I wasn't so sure. All I could say was I took the cards I was dealt, and tried to play my best hand. Was that to be my Personal Legend? Why couldn't I have some unique distinction or achievement to my name? It seemed unfair. All I craved was a modest token of achievement. Now I could see my planned point of departure about 100 yards ahead on the right. I rotated my innertube slightly so I could paddle backward in that direction. As I did, however, something caught my eye off to the left and I vigorously paddled in that direction. Between a giant rock and some overhanging bushes was an object trapped against the bank. As I approached within about 10 feet, I saw exactly what it was: a purple wool shirt, snagged on a low-lying branch and fluttering with the cold water as it headed its way north to the French Broad River.

EPILOGUE

Greenbrier Chronicles is a series of vignettes, more or less in chronological order, about my personal struggle to discover some area of expertise and overarching meaning of my journey. Just as Santiago of The Alchemist sought to find his Personal Legend, I wondered how I would be remembered. Interspersed throughout these struggles are frequent references to environmental concerns, especially as it relates to water, pollution, and global warming. Despite the moralistic overtones of environmentalism, however, most of this story could be aptly described as a non-fiction autobiography with a twist. The encounters and activities described are based on real life experiences, minor variations in timing and names of individuals and other details notwithstanding. The final chapters involving the "Think Tank from Alpha Centauri" stretches that interpretation a good bit. Although presented as a mind game, the interaction with this think tank clearly dominates the essence of the chronicles. And the final chapter suggests that maybe it wasn't a mind game at all. So, what's going on? Clearly, I have used the template of my life's story as a format to discuss the most important pressing issues of our times: global warming and related concerns about water. In a sense it trumps my personal journey. So why didn't I confront this issue head on with a direct assault? And why did I seem to go easy at times on the contrarians by granting them a degree of credibility? Most climate scientists are in strong agreement. My experience is that direct confrontation doesn't work very well in these situations. Like many political issues, environmental concerns are highly polarizing. Direct confrontation, didactic lectures, and condescension don't solve the problem, and they tend to increase the polarization.

In *This Changes Everything*, Naomi Klein presents the struggle to control global warming as "Capitalism vs. the Climate." In other words, unrestrained capitalism could cause serious problems with pollution and anthropogenic warming. Decreasing greenhouses gases, the probable cause of warming, would at least initially put some restraints on capitalism. There are multiple self-serving rationalizations for backing either capitalism or climate science. A broad perspective and objectivity are essential. Most people tend to believe the explanations of climate and environmental concerns that are most compatible with their immediate welfare. If their thinking evolves at all, it is more likely to occur through stories and self-examination than from external pressuring. Perhaps these chronicles may induce someone to take a close look at the issues. *Greenbrier Chronicles* is a story of my personal journey with an agenda. My hope is to increase the credibility of those seeking to fight climate change by decreasing our emission of greenhouse gases and, at the same time, foster an appreciation of our water resources from a domestic, recreational and industrial point of view. If I happen to discover my Personal Legend in the process, so much the better.

These issues concerning climate change and environmental well-fare are certainly important enough to garner our deepest concern. As noted by Marshall McLuhan, "There are no passengers on spaceship earth. We are all crew." At some point, we must all realize that there is no guarantee that a superpower will save us from catastrophe.

SELECTED BIBLIOGRAPHY

Books

Bastardi, Joe. *The Climate Chronicles: Inconvenient Revelations You Won't Hear from Al Gore and Others*. Minneapolis, Minnesota: Relentless Thunder Press, 2018.

Bryant, Page. *The Spiritual Reawakening of the Great Smoky Mountains*. Waynesville, North Carolina: Mystic Mountain Center, 1994.

Bryson, Bill. *A Short History of Nearly Everything*. New York, New York: Broad Books of Crown Publishing Group, 2003.

Cardwell, Glen. *The Greenbrier Cove Story*. Sevierville, Tennessee: Insight Publishing, 2012.

_____*A Dream Fulfilled: A Story About Pittman Center*. Sevierville, Tennessee: Insight Publishing, 2012.

Carson, Rachel. *Silent Spring*. New York, NY, and Boston, Massachusetts: Marine Books Houghton Mifflin Harcourt, 1962.

Coelho, Paulo. *The Alchemist*, 25th Anniversary Edition. New York, New York: HarperCollins Publishers LLC, 1993.

Cotham, Steve. *The Great Smoky Mountains National Park*. Charleston, South Carolina: Arcadia Publishing, 2006.

Cottrell, Jeanette and William B. *An American Family in the Twentieth Century*. Knoxville, Tennessee: Independently published. 1987.

Dunn, Durwood. *Cades Cove: The Life and Death of a Southern Appalachian Community 1818-1937*. Knoxville, Tennessee: The University of Tennessee Press, 2000.

Fishman, Charles. *The Big Thirst: The Secret Life and Turbulent Future of Water*. New York, New York: Free Press Division of Simon & Schuster, Inc., 2012.

Fray, Calvin. *Climate Change: Reality Check Basic Facts and Logic That Prove the Assault on CO_2 is Both Wrong and Dangerous*. Independently published, 2020.

Gore, Al. *An Inconvenient Truth: The Planetary Emergency of Global Warming and What We Can Do About It*. New York, New York: Rodale Inc. and Viking of Penguin Group, 2006.

Harari, Yuval Noah. Sapiens. New York, New York: HarperCollins Publishers, 2016.

Klein, Naomi. *This Changes Everything: Capitalism vs. The Climate*. New York, New York: Simon & Schuster, 2014.

Martin, Rod Jr. *Climate Basics: Nothing to Fear*. Cebu, Philippines: Tharsis Highlands Publishing, 2018, 2019.

Martin, William. *The Best Liberal Quotes Ever*. Naperville, Illinois: Sourcebooks, Inc., 2004.

Moran, Alan, editor. *Climate Change: The Facts*. Woodsville, New Hampshire: Stockade Books, 2015.

Pittman Center Alumni Association. *Pittman Community Center*. Sevierville, Tennessee: Insight Publishing, 1985.

Oreskes Naomi and Conway, Erik M. *Merchants of Doubt*. New York, New York and London, England, UK: Bloomsbury Press, 2011.

Pyne, Steve. *Fire: A Brief History*. Second Edition. Seattle, Washington: University of Washington Press, 2019.

Romm, Joseph. *Climate Change: What Everyone Needs to Know*. Second Edition. New York, New York: Oxford University Press, 2018.

Sapolsky, Robert M. *Behave*. New York, New York: Penguin Random House LLC, 2017.

Sedlak, David. *Water 4.0: The Past, Present, and Future of the World's Most Vital Resource*. New Haven, Connecticut and London: Yale University Press, 2014.

Singer, Fred and Avery, Dennis T. *Unstoppable Global Warming Every 1,500 Years*. Lanham, Maryland: The Rowman and Littlefield Publishing Group, Inc., 2007.

Smil, Vaclav. *Energy and Civilization: A History*. Cambridge, Massachusetts: The MIT Press, 2017.

Soloman, Steven. *Water: The Epic Struggle for Wealth, Power, and Civilization*. New York, New York: HarperCollins Publishers, 2015.

Sykes, Keith and Bunker, John. *Anesthesia and the Practice of Medicine*. London, United Kingdom: The Royal Society of Medicine Press, 2007.

Wallace-Wells, David. *The Uninhabitable Earth: A Story of the Future*. London and New York, New York: Penguin Random House UK and Crown Publishing Group, 2019.

Wood, Violet. *So Sure of Life: A Mountain Doctor's Story*. New York, NY: Friendship Press, 1999.

Wrightstone, Gregory. *Inconvenient Facts*. Allison Park, Pennsylvania: Silver Crown Productions LLC, 2017.

Articles

Beitler, Stu. "Powellton, WV Locomotive Explosion." *Chester Times*, Pennsylvania (December 27, 1934).

Fesenthal, Edward. "The Choice." *Time* (December 23/30, 2019).

Heron, Leigh Ann. "Archeological Field Work." *Smokies Life Magazine* (Spring, 2018, Volume 12, Number 1).

Mead, Rebecca. "Going for the Cold." *The New Yorker* (January 27, 2020).

Ross, Alex. "The Past and the Future of the Earth's Oldest Trees." *The New Yorker* (January 13, 2020).

About the Author

William M. Cottrell is a retired anesthesiologist who practiced medicine for more than 39 years in the area of Concord, North Carolina. In 2016, he authored his debut work, *Confessions of an Anesthesiologist,* and *Greenbrier Chronicles* picks up where his first book left off—the onset of retirement.

Cottrell grew up in the Knoxville, Tennessee area. He graduated from the University of Tennessee in 1971 with a BS in Chemistry with high honors. He received his MD degree from Emory in Atlanta, where he also served as student representative to the Southern Medical Association annual convention in 1973. He completed his residency in anesthesia at the University of Florida Teaching Hospitals in Gainesville, Florida, in 1978.

Cottrell has served in a variety of capacities in the medical community, including President of Cabarrus County Medical Society, Chairman of the Department of Anesthesia, and as a medical examiner for Cabarrus County. In addition to his love of writing, he enjoys playing acoustic guitar, golf, and physical fitness activities including hiking and swimming in the Greenbrier area. He enjoys a rich family life with his wife Rebecca, three children, two stepchildren, and six grandchildren plus one on the way.